Need You Now

A Pelican Bay Novella

MARIA K. ALEXANDER

MKA PRESS

Also By Maria K. Alexander

PELICAN BAY SERIES

You're Still the One

Need You Now

TANGLED HEARTS SERIES

Untangle My Heart

Forever in My Heart

Awaken My Heart

Believe in My Heart

Dedication

"True friends are never apart, maybe in distance but never in heart."
~ Unknown ~

To my friends near and far and the memories we've made together.

Chapter One

*"Courage doesn't mean you
don't get afraid. Courage means
you don't let fear stop you."*
~ Bethany Hamilton

THE AIR WAS SULTRY, humid, and ripe for a storm. Lightning lit up the sky, followed by the boom of thunder several seconds later. The weather forecasters had called for a tropical storm along the entire East Coast—a superstorm, they labeled it—and based on the way the rain slashed against the windows, they were spot-on.

The air conditioner unit in the window barely cooled off the apartment. Connor Maguire had stripped off his T-shirt and unbuttoned his shorts when there was a knock at the door. Two quick knocks followed by three slower.

Finally.

He opened the door and smiled down at the brown-haired beauty on the other side. *"Thought you'd never get here, darlin'."*

"Took longer because the whole damn town's crazy about this storm."

Connor grabbed the paper bag out of her hands and stepped back so she could enter. The wind blew hard, causing the door to slam wide open.

Was it his imagination, or did the air feel different from other storms?

Abby O'Connell swept in, her long, dark tresses held up in a drenched and sagging ponytail.

Connor peeked in the bag, smiling at the six-pack of his favorite brew. "No worries. Cade lent us his place for the night. We have food, weed, and beer. All the essentials to hunker down for the night."

She slipped out of her sandals and dropped her large tote bag onto the floor. "I'm soaked."

He took in her short sundress—a cute one in light blue with tiny white flowers—plastered to her body and molded to her luscious curves.

Grabbing her around the waist, he pulled her close. "It's not good to stay in wet clothes. Why don't I help you out of this?"

He moved his hands up her back and slid the zipper down. The cold from her wet dress did nothing to cool his temperature. And the points of her nipples as they pressed through the sheer fabric of her bra against his bare chest only added to his internal heat, causing an inferno of blood to flow to his cock.

Abby shoved at his shorts, pulling down his boxers at the same time. "Now you're talking."

Connor pushed the rest of her dress down and quickly rid Abby of her bra and thong, admiring her tanned body, firm breasts, and long legs.

Reaching into the brown bag, he pulled out two beers, cracked them open, and handed her one. "Here's to getting this party started."

They clinked cans and collapsed onto the couch, bodies intertwined with eager mouths and restless hands. Connor cupped her full breasts, swiping his thumbs over the hard peaks. With practiced expertise, she straddled him, taking him inside her in one slow stroke. They both moaned, and Connor thrust up in a matching rhythm as she rode him.

Hard.

She cried out his name as she climaxed.

Connor woke with a start, bathed in sweat and with a boner so hard it hurt.

Same damn dream...again.

Almost every night for the past few weeks. Ever since he'd run into Abby O'Connell on the Pelican Bay Boardwalk while she protested the Erickson Amusement Pier expansion. They'd barely spoken then, but based on the daggers she cast his way, she was not over their breakup from almost a decade ago.

They'd started dating his last year of high school, when her family moved to the small beach town of Pelican Bay, NJ. Abby grew up in Philadelphia and was used to a faster crowd than what the sleepy beach town provided. Connor had been looking for fast and wild, and Abby had been like no other girl he'd ever known, giving him both.

It had been years since he allowed himself to think about Abby.

He still had yet to meet another girl as special.

With a frustrated groan, he swung his legs off the bed and headed to the bathroom to seek relief that only came by his hand or a cold shower. After taking care of business, he dried off and returned to the bedroom. A quick glance at the clock showed it was a little past five a.m.; too late to go back to sleep, and too early to get his donut fix at Shore to Please Donuts.

After dressing in board shorts and a swim shirt, Connor walked through the apartment he lived in above Maguire Brother Renovations, the business he and his younger brother, Jason, started in Tampa. After returning to

Pelican Bay a couple months ago, they'd stayed and opened a new location of MBR.

The apartment wasn't much, but was the first place Connor had lived alone and didn't share a bathroom with anyone. It was a feeling he could get used to.

Opening the surf app on his smartphone, he checked the morning's conditions and found them marginally acceptable. It wouldn't be until fall before the waves got really good, but they were decent enough today. He tossed a towel, wetsuit, and other gear into a backpack, then grabbed his surfboard and exited the private stairs to the street.

He walked along Crocus Ave, the primary shopping district on the island. Although quiet in the predawn light, it would bustle with activity in an hour or two, once the sun rose and the businesses that catered to the breakfast crowd opened.

As he passed Shore to Please Donuts, he caught the glow of lights and inhaled the sugary scent of donuts and other freshly baked pastries. If he wasn't having sex, at least he could have donuts. He made a mental note to stop on his way home.

At Sixteenth Street, he turned right and headed toward the ocean. A couple of blocks later, he crossed over Ocean Ave and jogged up the ramp of the boardwalk, hurrying across to the stairs to the beach. Toeing off his shoes, he trekked across the sand until he reached the water's edge. He inhaled deeply, the scent of salt from the water filling his veins with energy and bringing a smile to his lips.

Tossing his gear on the sand, he tugged on his wetsuit. He grabbed his board, then ran into the water and dove into an oncoming wave. Breaking the surface, he smiled. Life didn't get any better than this.

Abby O'Connell had woken before dawn—again—after another restless night. With a week left before the grand opening of her soap shop, she had a million things to do and not enough hours in the day. Most nights she crashed in exhaustion after midnight, only to wake after a few hours and stare at the ceiling.

Usually, she woke with new tasks for her growing to-do list. But today the cause of her restlessness came in the form of a green-eyed, six-foot, sandy-haired ghost from her past named Connor Maguire. They'd dated on and off a solid three years after her family moved to Pelican Bay thirteen years ago.

Abby had been ticked when her mom moved them out of Philly, where there was always something to do, to the sleepy beach town.

And right before Abby's senior year!

Back then, Abby had a lot of attitude and resentment toward everything. When she was four, her dad died from an undetected brain aneurysm that burst. In the blink of an eye, her perfect family had been permanently changed.

Forced to sell their house in Northeast Philly to cover expenses, her mom had moved Abby and her two sisters into a two-bedroom apartment near the hospital off Broad Street in the heart of Philly, where she worked as a nurse.

It wasn't ideal, but over time they'd adjusted. When the girls got older and no longer needed help from the part-time nanny she hired, her mom switched to working the overnight shift, which left Abby's older sister, Natalie, in charge of watching them in the evening. Unfortunately, Nat wasn't the best role model and used to leave Abby in charge of their younger sister, Olivia, while Nat went clubbing.

That stopped when Natalie got knocked up at eighteen. She kept the baby, and while much about their life got complicated, Abby's nephew, Liam, quickly became the focus of all four O'Connell ladies.

Abby's mom wanted a better life for all of them...one outside the city. A patient told her about the wonderful times she'd had at Pelican Bay on vacation. Her mom took the family for a day trip, fell in love with the town, and hadn't looked back.

Which was how Abby found herself in a new town her senior year of high school.

Connor had been the perfect combination of hotness and trouble that Abby had been looking for to rebel against the move. He wasn't afraid to take chances and lived life to the fullest, from surfing to partying.

After his multiple failed attempts at asking her out during her first week at school, she ran into him on the beach late one day after school, where he'd been surfing. Sitting on the sand, she watched him for a while, admiring the way his long, lean body moved in tune with the waves. When he'd had his fill, he set his board down and dropped into the sand beside her.

"Ever surfed?" he asked.

"Kinda hard when living in a city," she snapped.

"You've never been to the shore before?"

"Of course I have, but I'm more of the lie-out-and-tan type."

"Right." He unzipped his wetsuit and peeled it down his chest, revealing a flat stomach with enough muscles to make Abby notice. "I could teach you."

Abby stared as he brushed the water off his face, the droplets sliding onto his perfect torso. Down, down they slid, past his belly button and beyond. The rush of wanting surprised her. She was no virgin, but the sex with the two boys from her old school hadn't been memorable or lasted more than a couple of weeks. And after Nat got pregnant, Abby had learned to keep her hormonal urges at bay.

Seeing Connor with his shaggy, beach-blond-streaked hair, smiling eyes, and ripped bod caused those urges to wake up.

"I don't have a surfboard," she said, and wiggled her toes in the sand.

"I have one you could borrow."

She shrugged in response.

He leaned forward, and for a quick second Abby thought—and kinda hoped—he was going to kiss her. "I'm here the same time most evenings, if you're interested." He gave her a sexy grin before standing and picking up his board. "See you around, Abby."

He walked away, the backside of him as perfect as the front.

Abby showed up the next day and every day after.

Shaking her head to clear away the memory, Abby rose from the bed and went into the bathroom. There'd be no more sleep, so she may as well start her day.

She quickly dressed in running shorts, a tank top, and sneakers. After grabbing a bottle of water, she went downstairs and let herself out the rear entrance, refusing to walk through the store and the reminder of all that needed to be done.

There'd be time to freak about work later. Now she needed to clear her head.

The benefit of living above her storefront was its prime location along the boardwalk, only a few steps away from the beach. Abby veered left and jogged along the water, pacing herself. She did a circuit around the lighthouse before turning and heading past where she started and the newly renovated amusement pier.

The sun had peeked past the horizon and was slowly making its way into a new day. Watching the sun rise over the Atlantic was one thing she'd missed most after leaving Pelican Bay nine years ago, a year after Hurricane Samantha hit and wrecked the small New Jersey barrier island. In the months since she'd returned, Abby had made a point of watching it rise every day. Each sunrise looked different and brought her a joy she'd experienced nowhere else.

Usually, she had this part of the beach to herself, but she caught the outline of someone in the water.

A surfer.

Her heart lurched as she got closer.

Could it be...

It was hard to be sure from the distance, but once he rose on the board and got into position, Abby recognized the form...the body...the man.

Connor Maguire.

After riding the wave in, he grabbed the board and paddled out even further. He straddled the board with his back to the shoreline, like a god calling to the waves. Then, with the ease and swiftness of the boy she remembered, he turned and paddled toward shore, rising at the perfect moment to get the lift and rush he needed to propel him forward.

Abby continued to run, mesmerized by his form, by the way his hair and body looked against the backdrop of the rising sun. The damn man was as beautiful as ever.

Despite the magnetic pull, she had every intention of running past him.

If only she had been watching where she was going.

When she stepped on something in the sand that caused her ankle to turn, all she could do was cry out as her knee buckled, and she started to fall.

Chapter Two

Connor sat astride his surfboard and took in the rising sun while he waited for the next swell. The rim of the yellow orb was visible just above the ocean. Shades of orange stretched along the horizon, as though it was giving the earth a warm embrace to welcome a new day.

He'd missed this...missed living minutes from the beach and being able to take in his fill of it every day. Having lived in Tampa the past ten years, Connor had access to beaches, but nothing beat having one practically in his backyard.

Since moving back, Connor had started each day jogging on the beach or surfing. Occasionally, he'd mix it up with yoga. All part of his lifestyle to keep his mind focused and clear. Daily physical exercise had been required when he was in rehab nine years ago for a substance abuse disorder. The first three weeks of his forty-five-day stint had been hell, but once he got through the worst of the withdrawal, he'd felt different...alive, with an appreciation of life he'd never had while high.

Now, he was a new man with a new purpose in life. And he intended to make good on all the promises he'd made to his family and, more importantly, to himself.

There was no going backward...only forward.

At the start of a swell, he flipped onto his stomach and paddled with long, even strokes. When he felt the lift of the wave, he popped up, landing in a crouch on both feet, his arms outstretched to maintain balance. The rush and buildup as the wave propelled him toward shore flowed through him as though he was one with the wave...the ocean. Like Poseidon, who could control the water and waves with a flick of his trident.

As the wave broke, he saw a girl running on the beach, her dark ponytail bouncing behind her. He was preparing to go back out for another ride when the girl stumbled, and she went down.

With no lifeguards on duty, the beach was empty. When the girl stayed on the ground, not moving, Connor paddled toward shore, grabbed his board, and ran out of the water.

Dropping his board in the sand, he kneeled next to the girl, who had sat up and was holding on to her ankle. "You okay?"

The girl lifted her chin and squinted in the sunlight. "I'm fine," she snapped.

Abby.

"You're hurt, Abby," Connor said. "Let me see your ankle."

She pulled it closer to her body. "Back off, Connor."

He knew her enough not to push, even though he could see shreds of pain beyond the pissed-off female attitude.

"I'm just trying to help."

"Well, I don't need your help."

He rose, not in the mood for a fight, especially with her. "Fine. Good luck walking in the sand with a sprained ankle."

"Go to hell."

Connor snorted. "Already been there, darlin'. No plans to go back."

He walked a few steps and bent down to get his board. He'd hoped since he moved back that they could talk and clear the air between them. Unresolved things based on his being an asshole as a kid. While he still had his share of screw-ups, he liked to think he'd learned a thing or two.

One of which was to ask for forgiveness.

Based on her scowl, Abby definitely was not in a forgiving state of mind.

He turned his back and walked away, only to pause when she cried out.

She must have gotten up and fallen again, because she still lay on the ground, but several feet away from where he'd found her. It took all of his control to ignore her and move to his backpack lying in the sand.

Slinging the bag over his shoulder and grabbing his board, he made his way toward the boardwalk, but she called out to him.

"Connor, wait."

He stopped but didn't turn around.

"Don't leave me," she called.

The familiarity of the words slammed into him, reminding him of another time when she'd said them.

"What do you mean you're leaving Pelican Bay? You can't go. Don't leave me, Con."

He shook away the memory and focused on the here and now. You couldn't change the past, only learn from it and make better decisions in the future.

Time to take his own advice.

Backtracking, he stopped a few feet away from where she still sat in the sand. The tide must have come up, as now her shorts and tank top were wet and plastered to her body. He wanted to point out she wouldn't have gotten covered in wet sand if she'd taken him up on his offer to help. Smarter to hold his tongue and wait for her to make the next move.

They stared each other down until she finally lowered her eyes to her ankle. "I can't walk on it."

"It's starting to swell."

A wave crashed and wet her again, this time splashing her face.

She grabbed a fistful of wet sand and threw it at the retreating water.

He bit back a laugh. She was sweaty, wet, pissed off as hell, and had never looked more beautiful to him.

"Don't you dare laugh at me, Connor Maguire."

"The thought never crossed my mind."

She snorted. "You're full of shit."

"What do you want, Abby?"

Their gazes held with the complexity of the fully loaded question until her shoulders dropped.

"I need help."

He cupped a hand to his ear. "What was that?"

"Don't be a shit. I need your help to stand."

"Was that a request or a demand?"

She let out a loud sigh. "Oh, for heaven's sake. Can you please help me up and get me back to my shop?"

He smiled, remembering how she hated asking for anything. She'd always been stubborn...never wanting to show she was vulnerable. It had both driven him crazy and turned him on at the same time.

In response, he slid his arm through the other strap of his backpack. Bending down, he picked her up and cradled her close to his chest. He hadn't been prepared for the jolt when he touched her. Or the effect the familiar smell of her coconut shampoo had on him. She flinched, which made him think—or maybe hope—she felt it too.

"What about your board?"

"Hold on to my neck."

She hesitated a moment before complying, and he had to push aside the groan that had been building inside him.

With her in his arms, he lowered and grabbed his board. Carrying both her and the board, he walked through the sand to the boardwalk.

Abby couldn't believe her bad luck. First for jogging on the beach at the same time Connor was surfing. Then to fall and twist her ankle while ogling him. To be fair, it was hard not to stare. Watching him surf had been a favorite pastime of hers when they'd dated...even before they'd dated. Hell, it had been how he'd finally gotten a date with her.

But that was a long time ago, and Abby had changed a lot over the years. She'd gone to college for chemistry, specializing in cosmetics, and worked at a major cosmetic manufacturer in Texas for a couple of years, before returning to Pelican Bay three months ago to open her own handmade soap and skincare shop.

Since owning a business involved more than making the products, Abby had taken a couple of basic business classes. Her sister, Natalie, had also agreed to invest—a.k.a. sign her name on the small business loan—and together they were trying to launch this new business.

The last thing Abby needed was a sprained ankle to slow her down...or the distraction of a sexy six-foot surfer.

Connor carried her and his surfboard effortlessly, even though she stood only a few inches shorter than him. When they reached her shop, he put her down so she could remove her key from the pocket of her running shorts and unlock the door.

Stale, barely cool air greeted them, along with a disorganized mess of display cases, ladders, and paint cans. Abby hopped inside, holding on to the doorframe for support until she reached a ladder to lean on.

"Looks like a war zone in here," he said, laying his surfboard and bag outside the door.

"We'd just started painting when they delivered the counters and display tables. Now it's making it harder to paint," Abby said.

In truth, they would have finished the painting last week if she and Nat hadn't had to move their younger sister, Olivia, into an apartment. Livvie had recently finished school for physical therapy and taken a job working in a rehab center for one of the major hospitals in Philly.

"What kind of store are you opening?" Connor asked.

"One that sells homemade soaps, lotions, and skincare."

"You make them?"

"I do. That so surprising?" she snapped.

He shook his head, dried strands of hair sticking out in a sexy shag. "Not at all. You always talked about wanting to start your own skincare business. I remember the candles and soaps you used to make."

Abby avoided his gaze, remembering how they'd used the soaps on each other many times.

"When are you opening?"

"In a week."

He eyed the interior skeptically before fixing those beautiful green eyes on her. "Let's check out your ankle."

"I'm sure it's fine," she said, even though it throbbed like a son-of-a-bitch.

"Let me be the judge of that."

"Since when are you a doctor?"

"I've seen plenty of injuries on the job. Jace and I have had to patch up ourselves and guys who work for us so we could get the job done."

She huffed out a breath. "There's an area in the back where we can go."

Before she could stop him, he once again lifted her off her feet and zigzagged his way around the chaos and through the doorway. The large, open room would serve as a work area for making products and as a stockroom. Unopened boxes of shelving stood propped against the wall waiting to be assembled. Only then could they unpack the boxes of stock and supplies piled in a disorganized mess.

Connor set her down on a folding chair near the kitchen area. Grabbing another chair, he elevated her injured foot and removed her running shoe. With gentle hands, he stroked along her right ankle, his touch both arousing and tickling her.

"I'd say it's a minor sprain. You have a first-aid kit?"

"In the bathroom." She gestured to a small room off to the side.

He disappeared and returned with a red plastic box. Rummaging inside, he grabbed an ice pack, cracked it to activate it, and pressed it on her ankle. The coolness was a welcome relief against her hot skin, although she didn't know if she was warm because of her injury or because of the man.

Finding an antiseptic pad, he cleaned a scrape she hadn't realized she had on her knee. She flinched when he blew on it to ease the sting, the feel of his warm breath on her skin causing her heart to skip a few beats.

What the hell was wrong with her?

After adding antibiotic ointment, he covered it with a bandage. Then he moved to her right hand, which also had a slight scrape, and started the same process.

"You should try to keep your foot elevated and iced over the next twenty-four hours. Fifteen minutes on, fifteen off," Connor said.

"I know how to take care of a sprained ankle."

"You can also take something mild with ibuprofen to help with the swelling," he continued.

She reached down to examine her ankle, which had puffed up like the time she was at Great Adventure and had a mild reaction from a bee sting.

Just what she didn't need.

"I've got it. I'll be fine," she mumbled.

He closed the box and returned it to the bathroom. When he didn't return right away, she went in search of him, wincing as her ankle protested.

She found him in the front room of the store. He'd removed the wetsuit and now stood in navy board shorts. She stared at his bare back, more muscled than she remembered, and even more enticing.

"This is a great space," he said. "Who's going to finish the painting and other things before you open?"

"Natalie is helping me. We're partners," she said.

"Right." He bent over and picked up a paint tray with semi-dried paint and a stiff roller.

She winced. Truth be told, Natalie had the best intentions of helping but had issues with time management. And apparently cleaning up painting supplies.

"Your ankle may slow you down. I wouldn't climb a ladder or put full pressure on it for a couple of days," Connor said.

Was he crazy? Everything she had to do involved putting pressure on both her feet.

"I'll be fine. A little ice, a couple Advil, and I'll be good as new."
She hoped.

He set down the ruined paint tray and rummaged in his backpack, pulling out a business card. Finding a pen on a counter, he scribbled something and handed it to her.

"My number. Let me know if you need any help."

"I don't need your help, Con. I've got this."

He shrugged in a careless way that never failed to drive her crazy and pressed the card into her hand.

"I'll get going, then." He opened the door, slung the backpack strap over a bare shoulder, and held up the surfboard. "See you around, Abby."

Then he was gone, and she was alone with an empty space in both her store and her heart.

Chapter Three

CONNOR RETURNED TO HIS apartment, showered, and had started the Keurig when the front door opened, and Jason entered, carrying a white pastry box.

With the morning's chaos, Connor had forgotten to get donuts. During his walk home, he couldn't get his mind off Abby with her sad brown eyes, standing amidst a renovation disaster.

"Mornin', bro," Jason called out.

"Hey. You were reading my mind," Connor said, and popped in a second coffee pod.

"Can't have a meeting without sugar to go with our caffeine."

"You know it."

They'd closed on the Pelican Bay location of Maguire Brothers Renovations a week ago. Since then, he and Jace had worked tirelessly on the renovations. The advantage of buying older buildings was you could get them for dirt cheap. The downside was many of them had the original of everything, and required a full overhaul.

Jace and he had a system that started with a morning meeting over breakfast, where they touched base on projects and discussed each of their plans for the day. After, they'd spend a couple hours working on their place, before moving to other work.

Going into business with his brother had been the best thing he'd done. Connor's life had been in a serious tailspin when his mom moved him and Jace to Tampa after Hurricane Samantha nearly destroyed Pelican Bay almost ten years ago. The two-bedroom bungalow his family had rented at the south end of the town was only a block from the beach and had sustained too much water damage to be livable. With no savings, his father MIA, and nowhere to live, his mom reached out to her brother, Tom, who offered to put them up while they figured out their next step.

The first year in the Sunshine State had resulted in Connor spending two stints in rehab for a substance abuse disorder that had started in high school. The forced rehab had given him nothing but time to evaluate his life and figure out what he wanted. After he got through the worst part, he'd realized there was more to life than partying and his next fix. He'd been clean ever since.

Once released after the second round of rehab, he focused on working with Jason at a construction company. Sure, sometimes the temptation for a quick fix crept in, but Connor learned to recognize the signs and would fit in a meeting or call his sponsor. He also communicated to his brother when he was feeling edgy. Jace was a tremendous support and would listen if Connor wanted to unload his worries or join him in a yoga class.

When they'd saved enough, they'd started their own business flipping houses. A few years later, they'd gotten noticed by a TV network and received an offer to host a home improvement show called *Beach House Flippers*.

Their reputation at flipping houses, along with a desire to help their hometown, was what brought them back to Pelican Bay a few months ago.

Thanks to the resources from *Beach House Flippers*, they'd filmed a season of the show around renovating Erickson Fun Pier, which had sustained serious damage in the storm.

Damage including loss of the Sun Jet roller coaster, which had fallen into the Atlantic when the boardwalk gave way to the storm. Connor remembered the intensity of the storm and the shock when he learned about the coaster's demise, including that his brother and friends had been on the pier when it happened. Tyler Erickson and Maddy Kinkaid had been on the coaster when it fell and would likely have died if it hadn't been for Mr. Erickson, who saved them, even though it cost him his life.

The amusement pier renovation was a key step in rebuilding in order to entice tourists to the barrier island. Once a prime vacation spot for families, the thirty-block town of Pelican Bay had suffered major damage and not recovered. The hype from having *Beach House Flippers* film on the island had brought awareness to the town and awakened a new interest in not only Pelican Bay but also other small towns along the Jersey coast.

With the pier complete, the brothers turned their attention to other much-needed renovations. Now, Connor and Jason were full-fledged Pelican Bay business owners, having set down roots in their hometown. They'd bought this house to set up as HQ for their business, plus a couple of other properties, including the development where their old house was, and the mini-golf place that had once been the hot spot for kids and families.

"Jenna can't make our morning meeting. Her boxes are arriving from Florida, and she needs to let the movers into her apartment," Jason said, reading a text from his phone.

Jenna was one of Uncle Tom's kids and several years younger than Connor and Jace. Both she and her brother, Kyle, worked at the Maguire Brothers' Tampa office. Jenna had offered to move to Pelican Bay to get their new location up and running. She was a godsend, handling everything, including speaking with prospective customers, helping manage their schedules and project timelines, getting permits, and assessing potential properties. Whatever they needed, Jenna handled, which allowed Connor and Jason to focus on the actual renovation work.

Connor carried two cups of coffee into the partially complete conference room, which served as their war room. Their first order of business after they bought the space had been to replace the flooring. Now the wide, dark gray planks gave the place a modern look. Framing of the offices and conference rooms was complete, and installation of the drywall was in progress. Thankfully, they were used to working despite the construction zone. Another few days to finish the drywall and they could start painting.

Which reminded Connor of Abby and the painting mess at her place.

Jason removed an apple cider donut from the box. "You surf this morning?"

"Yeah. Conditions were decent." Connor followed suit and bit into the warm, sweet deliciousness of the most perfect donut ever. Over the years, he'd replaced drugs with sweets, which meant he had to work his ass off to stay fit. Thankfully, his job helped in that area.

"Let me know next time you're going."

Connor raised an eyebrow. "You'll leave your love nest with Emma to surf?"

Jason pulled the pastry box toward him and away from his brother. "Emma doesn't have a problem when I surf or jog with your sorry ass in the morning."

Connor chewed the last bite of donut and swallowed. "She was probably on her second cup of coffee and already working on her laptop."

"She's more relaxed with the pier opening behind us. Besides, I have excellent distraction techniques to keep her mind off work." Jason waggled his eyebrows.

He had reunited with his high school sweetheart when they returned to Pelican Bay. Now, the couple were planning a wedding and preparing to renovate Emma's grandparents' seventy-five-year-old Victorian home, which she inherited when her grandmother passed away earlier in the year.

After their crappy childhood, no one deserved to be happy more than Jace. Still, a part of Connor envied his brother's relationship and the future with the woman he loved.

What would have happened if Connor had never left Pelican Bay? Would he and Abby have made things work?

He shook his head to clear the useless thoughts. Abby had made it clear on more than one occasion she wanted nothing to do with him.

"You okay, bro?" Jason asked.

By now, his brother knew how to tell when things were weighing on his mind. And who better to ask for advice than from someone who overcame his own obstacles to find love?

"I ran into Abby today at the beach."

Jace raised an eyebrow. "She surfing?"

"Running. She tripped and fell. Twisted her ankle."

"She okay?"

"She couldn't walk on it. I helped her to her shop and got ice for her. It's no big deal."

Connor could feel his brother watching him.

"I know how close you were, so I think it *is* a big deal. What aren't you telling me?"

"Her ankle is banged up pretty good. Her shop is opening in a week, and inside is a disaster. Dried paint trays, crap everywhere."

Jace leaned back in his chair and smiled. "You want to help her."

Connor hated admitting it, but his brother was spot-on, as usual. "I offered. She won't let me."

"Since when has a stubborn female gotten the better of you?"

"Hello. It's Abby. Have you forgotten how stubborn she is?"

"You can be pretty damn stubborn yourself."

"It's different now."

"Why?"

Connor pushed a hand through his hair. "I guess because I'm different. I'm not the kid she dated, who was constantly stoned and looking for a good time."

"And?"

"What if she doesn't like me this way?"

"You're selling yourself and Abby short, man. Let her get to know a different side of you."

Could he take his brother's advice, or was he better off staying clear of Abby the way she wanted? Or maybe she didn't want him to stay away and was too afraid—or proud—to admit it?

Too many possibilities to think about this early in the day. Connor grabbed a second donut, one of the few things in his life that was welcoming and never let him down.

Abby showered and dressed without putting too much pressure on her injured ankle. Opting to let her hair air dry rather than blowing out the waves, she grabbed coffee and a Greek yogurt, and ate her breakfast while icing her ankle.

She texted Natalie to see when she would arrive. They had a lot to do, and despite what she'd told Connor, Abby wasn't sure how much physical work she'd be able to accomplish with her injury. Natalie worked full time at the Pelican Bay General Store and picked up a few shifts at Tonino's Pizza and Pasta on weekends. She'd given her notice at the General Store, but with another couple of days of work remaining, the brunt of the preparation for the grand opening had fallen on Abby's shoulders.

Poor planning.

Downstairs, Abby limped to the thrift-store desk she'd bought dirt cheap and booted up her laptop. They'd placed advertisements in the local papers for a June seventh opening—a little off the mark from the Memorial Day opening she'd hoped for.

Paper tote bags, business cards, and other promotional materials with the Soap Sisters logo had arrived two days ago and were sitting in boxes. Now, if only they could make headway on the painting, Abby would feel less stressed. Boxes of pretty gray laminate wood flooring sat stacked along a wall. Given their slow progress with painting, Abby was rethinking tackling the flooring until after prime tourist season was over at the end of the summer. At the rate they were progressing, they'd be lucky to finish the painting before opening.

She needed help with the handiwork.

Call Connor.

Abby picked up the business card he'd left, turning it over to finger the number he'd written.

My number. Let me know if you need any help.

His words were tempting. Regardless of their past, Connor would help if she asked. And hadn't he already offered?

No.

She set the card on the desk. She needed to do this on her own.

Abby had dreamed of opening a shop for years. She'd learned about production, packaging, and distribution while working for a cosmetics company, and planned to leverage her knowledge along with the product line she'd been perfecting.

After a visit home to Pelican Bay a few months ago, and learning the town was preparing to put serious money into renovating the boardwalk, including restoring Erickson Fun Pier, Abby had decided it was time to take a chance on her new business.

An enticing offer had been made to new business owners, including a reduced rent the first year and a lesser discount the second year. After discussing the idea with her mom and Natalie, the sisters signed a two-year lease, with the option to renew.

Erickson Fun Pier had reopened a week ago. Every day since had brought a noticeable increase in visitors to the beach town, especially along the boardwalk. Abby needed to capitalize on the bump in tourists.

But first, they needed to finish the renovations.

The bell on the front door of the store jingled, which meant Nat had arrived. Abby limped to the doorway leading to the main area of the store.

"Hey, sis. What happened?" Nat asked, taking in the ice pack Abby had taped to her ankle.

"Stepped in a hole while jogging on the beach."

"Wow. How bad is it?"

"It's swollen, but I don't think it's broken. Hurts like a bitch, though."

"Maybe we should have Mom check it out or get it x-rayed."

Abby shook her head. "There's no time. Besides, someone saw me fall and confirmed it's a sprain."

Natalie raised an eyebrow. "Who?"

"Connor." Abby hobbled over to grab the dried-up paint pan and tossed it into a trash bag. She so did not want to have this conversation.

"Connor Maguire?"

"He was surfing and got a firsthand view of my fall."

"Huh." Natalie studied her sister. "And?"

"And nothing."

"Abs, this is the first time you've been close to Connor in forever. It wasn't weird?"

Weird was an understatement.

Abby avoided her sister's gaze. "He helped me back here and got me an ice pack. No big deal."

"I call bullshit," Natalie said. "Connor was the one who got away, right? And now you're telling me being up close and personal with him is no big deal?"

"Drop it, Nat."

Natalie laughed. "I've seen his home improvement show. He's even hotter than he was when you were together. You had to feel *something*."

"I'm over Connor." Abby picked up a plastic drop cloth. "Let's get to work. This place isn't going to paint itself."

"Fine, ignore me. I forgot I'm talking to the Queen of Denial." Natalie helped Abby spread out the cloth and move the ladder. "How are you going to paint with your ankle?"

"You paint the top, and I'll paint the bottom."

"Can you at least have Mom look at your ankle?"

Abby huffed out a breath. "Fine. I'll text her later. Pinkie promise." She held out her pinkie to link like they used to do as kids.

Natalie turned on music, and they worked in tandem throughout the morning, stopping early afternoon for lunch. In front of the large picture window in Abby's apartment, they ate salads while taking in the scenery that overlooked the boardwalk and offered a prime view of the ocean.

Fluffy clouds dotted the clear blue sky, making it a perfect beach day. The Atlantic sat before their eyes in its full glory. The sun sparkled and reflected off the water, which moved with a synchronous grace as waves rose, crashed, and came into shore. Multicolored striped umbrellas adorned the beach, where families relaxed in equally colorful beach chairs. In the distance, Abby could see a pair of kids tossing a Frisbee and a father helping his son fly a kite.

From Abby's viewpoint, everyone was laughing and relaxing. Enjoying a day of fun in the sun.

She chugged the last of her iced tea. "You almost done?"

"What's your hurry?"

"Seven days to opening, Nat. That's all we have to be ready."

"I'm well aware, since you downloaded a countdown app on my phone, which reminds me each morning."

Abby rose and pointed out the window. "Look at all the people on the boardwalk and the beach. Those are all potential customers we're not engaging with, since we're not open."

"Then let's find a way to engage with them sooner."

"Any ideas how?"

"What if we hand out flyers and soap samples?" Natalie said.

Abby had been thinking along the same lines. "How, when we're working in here?"

"Maybe Liam can help."

"Aren't you always complaining about how he sleeps until lunch now that school's out and shows up late or blows off his job at Harrison's? Besides, it's soaps. What boy is going to want to hand out soaps?"

"It would only be until we open. Let me ask him."

"Okay, fine. See what he says."

Natalie's phone rang. While she answered it, Abby carried her bowl to the kitchenette and washed it. In the background, she could hear Natalie's voice rising, a clear sign something was wrong.

"For the love of God." Natalie stormed over with her own dish and started scrubbing. "I'm losing my mind with that child."

Abby frowned. "What's he done now?"

At the beginning of the school year, Liam had started hanging out with a new group of friends. To say it was a bumpy year was an understatement. There had been multiple incidents where Natalie was called by the school. It started with cutting classes and bullying others. Lately it had progressed to minor vandalism and drinking on the property late at night.

Abby braced herself for whatever new drama her sister faced.

"That was Ethan. He caught Liam and his friends smoking pot at the old mini-golf place," Natalie said.

Ethan Hunter graduated the year before Abby, and had done his own share of hell-raising in his teenage years. He'd gotten his act together, and now was part of Pelican Bay's law enforcement. He was a friend to the sisters and did his best to toe the line when it came to Liam and his shenanigans.

"Hell. Did he take him to the station?" Abby asked.

"He wasn't on duty. And since the new owner of the property didn't cause a problem, Ethan called me to pick up Liam."

"Someone bought old Mr. Riley's place?"

"The Maguire brothers bought it."

Right...of course they did. The town had been buzzing about the Maguire brothers since they returned to town for the pier renovation. Abby couldn't walk into the market without catching dribs of the local gossip, including speculations on which real estate the brothers would snatch up next.

Probably to spotlight on their TV show.

Natalie dried her hands and grabbed her bag off the counter. "I need to pick him up and deal with this. I'm sorry to bail on you."

"I understand."

"I'll call you later and try to come back before my shift at the store," Natalie said, and dashed out the front door.

Abby did understand, but whether it was a conference with a teacher, an injury during sports, or a fight at school, there was always drama Natalie had to deal with. It was one concern Abby had about starting a business with her sister.

Being a single mom was tough. Their mom had been a single parent for most of their life, and Abby was a witness to how hard it was to juggle a job and family demands. At fourteen, Liam needed to be accountable for his actions. But even the part-time job he'd gotten at Harrison's Market didn't seem to keep her nephew out of trouble.

In the main room of the store, Abby reviewed their progress and considered what she could accomplish on her own. With the left and back walls drying, she picked up where she left off on the right wall. Since she was doing her best not to use the ladder, she painted what she could reach with the roller brush.

Choosing her favorite ABBA playlist, she sang along with the music as she painted. She made her way to the wall facing the boardwalk and was moving the ladder off the plastic drop cloth when she stepped into a puddle of paint. Of course, she stepped in it with her injured foot. When she started sliding, she lunged for the ladder to stop herself from falling, but her reflexes weren't quick enough. Her feet slipped out from underneath her, and she crashed to the ground, the ladder falling on top of her.

Chapter Four

AFTER A MORNING INSTALLING drywall at the office with his brother, Connor grabbed lunch from Harrison's Market and drove to the lighthouse. One project they'd gotten approval from the town council to start was building the Pelican Bay Museum. With its location next to the lighthouse, it would offer visitors the history of the lighthouse and the island, including the tragic story of Hurricane Samantha and its impact on the town and the surrounding area.

Connor and Jason were waiting for the permits that would allow them to break ground for the construction. In the meantime, Connor wanted to get a head start on the nature trail they planned to build across from it. He'd spent his free time sketching the area and planning how they'd excavate the ground.

Rather than sitting at one of the picnic tables available for visitors, Connor walked to the rocks surrounding the lighthouse and settled himself on a relatively flat rock. Removing lunch from the bag, he bit into a corned beef and Swiss sandwich. The soft marble rye held the perfect balance of spicy mustard to meat and cheese ratio. He sighed in pleasure.

Having grown up with little money thanks to an alcoholic father who had a habit of drinking or gambling away their funds, Connor and Jason had often struggled to scrounge enough change to cover the reduced-fee lunch at school.

As a result, Connor appreciated food and took every opportunity to expand his palate and try different cuisine from a variety of cultures. Since returning to Pelican Bay, he'd been working his way through the restaurants, delis and grocery stores, always willing to try something new, along with his favorites.

He finished half the sandwich and was taking a swig of iced tea when someone called his name.

Emma Erickson, his soon-to-be sister-in-law, picked her way over the rocks.

"Hey, Connor," she said, dropping onto a rock and wiggling to find a comfortable spot.

"What's up, Emma?" He held out the bag of chips, and she snagged a few.

"Nice day. The breeze here is refreshing."

"The sound of the water against the rocks is relaxing. When I can, I like to come out here and eat lunch."

"Can't say I blame you."

They sat in silence, although Connor knew Emma wouldn't be able to sit for more than a few minutes. He'd never met someone who always seemed in motion, with a to-do list that rivaled a rolling social media feed.

"Jace mentioned you'd be here to prep for the nature trail," she said.

"Once it's marked out, we can start laying the trails and bringing in the shrubs and foliage to complement what's already here."

"It's going to be a great addition to this area. I hope it brings the pelicans back."

Pelican Bay had gotten its name because of a specific breed of pelican that inhabited this part of the island as far back as a hundred years ago. During a severe storm, a boat had gotten caught in the rocks and would have sunk if it hadn't been for the pelicans who guided the boat to the inlet of the island. The story of the rescue drew the attention of a developer, who built on the island and named it Pelican Bay. It had once been the home of many pelicans who stayed near the lighthouse and were believed to help guide boats through the inlet.

Connor remembered a few on this part of the island. He'd heard that after Hurricane Samantha, they hadn't been seen again.

"Hope so," he said.

"I received a call from our local scout troop. They've helped maintain this area throughout the years as part of their service projects. I thought they could help with building out the trail, or maybe build birdhouses you could hang along the trail," she said.

Connor was up for the free labor, but kids?

"How many are you talking about, and how old?" he asked

"About ten kids between thirteen and fifteen."

"Would there be any adults here with them?"

Emma laughed. "Of course. Their troop leader and a few parents would be here to help give them direction. It wouldn't all be on you."

"I guess it should be fine. Birdhouses, you're thinking?"

"Yes, and they can also dig holes for the plants or whatever else you need."

"Will I need to get supplies for the birdhouses?"

"The scout leader will take care of that. We'll need you or someone to provide direction for what you want them to do."

"How soon are you wanting to do this?"

"Is a day in the next couple of weeks too soon? Maybe in the midafternoon, when it's not as hot?"

"Should be fine. Give me a couple of days to figure out the timing."

They both stood.

"Perfect. Thanks, Connor. I need to get back to work. Why don't you come by for dinner tonight? We can barbecue, plus I made clam chowder."

Even though he'd just eaten, his mouth watered at the thought of Emma's clam chowder.

"Two of my favorites. Thanks."

He appreciated how often Emma included him at family dinners. With his own mom in Florida and Jace living at Emma's, Connor had a lot of time on his hands.

They climbed off the rocks and walked side by side toward the lighthouse.

"Come by around seven," Emma called, and waved as she headed to the parking lot.

Connor disposed of his trash and laid out the diagram of the area on a picnic table. After studying it, he returned to his truck and removed marking paint, wooden stakes, string, and a shovel. He spent an hour marking out the trail with stakes and string, making adjustments along the way.

Outdoor landscaping was his favorite part of a project. Whenever he and Jace flipped houses, Connor had always been in charge of putting together a design with the right combination of trees, shrubs, and flowers to make an enticing curb appeal. Trying different combinations and styles gave him a creative outlet he found relaxed him. Good thing, since it drove his brother crazy, which meant Connor got full creative control as long as he stuck to their budget.

After finishing all he could for the day and making notes for changes he wanted to tweak in the design, he stored his gear in the truck. It was midafternoon, and he didn't have any pressing business. He could catch up with Jason at one of their other properties, but he didn't feel like it.

Before he could talk himself out of a potentially bad idea, he drove to PB Coffee Shop and picked up two iced coffees and a half-dozen chocolate chip cookies in a clear bag marked with the Shore to Please logo. One of the things he'd forgotten about his hometown was how local businesses supported each other by selling each other's products in select stores. It was common to find items like pastries, candy, and saltwater taffy in a coffee shop or market.

Back in his truck, Connor drove into the lot behind Erickson Arcade and parked. Grabbing the coffees and cookies, he walked up the ramp to the boardwalk and over to Abby's store. As he raised his hand to knock, a loud crash came from the other side of the door.

Abby had always been a clumsy kid with more scrapes and cuts on her legs and arms than her sisters. Her mom used to laugh and say it was a good thing she was a nurse, because all three of her daughters kept her in a regular state of applying bandages and antibiotic ointment.

Now, as Abby lay halfway in the tray of paint, the ladder half covering her, she wondered if she'd made a wrong decision about starting her own business. Clearly, she couldn't do something as basic as paint. How could she sell her products to customers?

She scooted off the paint tray and did her best to slide out from under the ladder. Difficult, given her shorts and the right side of her lower half were drenched in paint.

Could her day get any worse?

The door jingled as it opened, and Connor appeared in the doorway. He wore a navy-blue Maguire Brothers Renovations T-shirt with khaki cargo shorts. With his hair windblown, like he'd driven with the windows down, he carried two iced drinks and a bakery bag.

She lifted her head to the sky and wondered what she'd done in life to make her have the worst luck in the world.

"Whoa, you all right?" Tossing his purchases on the counter, he hurried to remove the ladder from her.

Abby pushed a stray hair out of her face. "I'm fine. Just a new way I found to paint."

"Uh huh." He offered his hands to help her up.

She hesitated.

"Jesus, Abby."

Expelling the breath she'd been holding, she let him take her hands, nearly jumping at the spark from his touch.

As he guided her to her feet, she swayed, and he placed his hands on her waist to steady her. At five feet eight, she stood only a few inches shorter than him, which lined up their bodies perfectly. And right now, standing close to him, her body responded to being pressed up against his deliciously firm one.

Traitor.

When her legs buckled, he pulled her more firmly against him. It was impossible not to feel his arousal, and despite her own good sense—which was clearly on break—she lifted her eyes to meet his. The green irises bored into hers, dark with desire, and her arms naturally held on to his shoulders for support.

God, she'd forgotten how good it felt in his arms. All she had to do was lift her chin a fraction of an inch and she'd be able to taste him. The thought of pressing her mouth to his ignited a fiery desire within her.

His lips parted, as though he was going to kiss her.

Then he did something unexpected.

He leaned his forehead against hers—as though he was trying to gain control—before taking a deep breath and stepping back, keeping a loose hold on her waist.

"What happened to you not using a ladder?" he asked.

The distance and lack of his warmth against her was like being hit by an unexpected wave, and Abby pulled away, further separating her from his hold.

"Nat had been using it when she was here earlier. It fell onto me when I slid in paint." Now her face flushed with embarrassment. Not only had she fallen—again—she was covered in paint and had almost kissed Connor.

The day kept getting better and better.

"Why don't you get changed while I clean up here?"

She opened her mouth, prepared to argue, but gave up, since he'd started wiping the sodden plastic. Hobbling to the back room, she made her way to the area where the washer and dryer were located. When she'd first seen the space, the realtor mentioned the past owner had a toddler and installed a tiny laundry room on the main level to save her from running up and down the stairs all day.

Abby hadn't been living there more than a couple of months and had found it came in handy when cleaning up spills from making her products. The downside was that she had a tendency to forget to bring her clean clothes upstairs and often had to come downstairs in a towel to get underwear.

She pulled off her shorts and tossed them into the washbasin next to the appliances. Turning on the water, she rubbed at the paint, pleased to see it washing away. After wringing them out and hanging them over an empty basket, she used a washcloth to wipe at the paint on her legs.

She'd turned off the water and was drying her legs when her name was called. She opened her mouth to tell him to give her a minute, but it was too late.

There was a hiss and the sound of something dropping. Abby didn't have to turn to know he had found her.

"Really, Con. Getting changed here," she snapped.

He had the good sense to flush before picking up the brush he'd dropped and turning away.

But not before sweeping his eyes down her body and taking in her cropped T-shirt and thong.

Abby had never been a shy girl. Nudity didn't embarrass her, and normally she wouldn't have cared that he'd seen her practically bare ass.

Except it was Connor.

He knew what lay beneath those panties, and she remembered all too well what he'd done underneath the panties. And dammit if those memories didn't heat her blood again with want for him to take her down memory lane.

"Sorry. I was looking for a place to wash out the brushes because they're getting hard."

Wrong word to say as he stood there aroused, based on the bulge between his legs.

"Give me a second and you can use the sink." She reached into another basket and yanked out a pair of denim shorts. "Done," she said, fastening the button.

"This is where you create your skincare products?" he asked.

"Yes."

"Looks like a kitchen."

"Each product has a specific recipe. Some things have to be boiled or mixed, so we need burners, blenders, and pots, along with molds for the soaps."

"Pretty cool. How much do you make in advance?"

"The products last for a while, but I prefer to make small batches and keep things as fresh as possible." She pointed to the stacked boxes with shelving she'd purchased but hadn't yet put together. "As you can see, we're still getting ourselves organized. Soon I'll need to make stock for the opening."

Having finished washing the brushes, he followed her to the front. He inspected what she and Natalie had painted earlier. The pale blue-gray had dried to a color reminding Abby of a clear sky, the perfect combination of bright and welcoming.

"You're almost done," Connor said.

"Can't happen soon enough for me."

Connor picked up the two iced drinks and handed her one. "Then let's get it finished." He took a long swig of the drink and moved the drop cloth to a better position.

"What do you think you're doing?"

Grabbing the ladder, he positioned it over the front door, first locking it so no one could enter. "Helping you finish this wall."

"I didn't ask for your help, Connor."

"I'm offering my help."

"Why?"

"Does there need to be a reason?"

Abby eyed him suspiciously. With a wide smile that crinkled the corners of his eyes and a tan that showed the amount of time he spent in the sun, he reminded her of the boy she used to know. Except young Connor had always been ready for a good time...which didn't involve work. His motto had been "play before work."

The man standing before her looked like he worked more than played based on the muscles in his arms and clarity of his eyes. Dark blond locks streaked from the sun fell to the bottom of his neck with a hint of curl at the bottom. His firm jaw held a dusting of dark blond scruff. She didn't see any hidden agenda in his offer to help, but still...

"Cookie?" He held out the bakery bag.

She shrugged with feigned interest.

He reached in and pulled out a large chocolate chip cookie.

Her mouth watered as the scent of the sweet milk chocolate confection hit her.

"These were your favorite," he said, holding it out to her.

She hesitated a moment before giving in. "You're evil." She took the cookie, taking a large bite and doing her best not to moan at the sugary party in her mouth.

He watched her, studying her mouth as she chewed.

The jerk was flirting with her.

And worse, she was letting him—and liking it.

She swallowed and held up the index finger of her non-cookie hand. "One wall, Connor."

He saluted her. "Yes, ma'am."

He poured paint into a fresh tray—thankfully, she'd gotten disposable liners—grabbed a brush, and climbed the ladder with the can, giving her a view of his perfect, shorts-clad ass.

She took a sip of her iced coffee and took her time eating her cookie, savoring both the pastry and the view.

Chapter Five

CONNOR DROVE THE SPEED limit to Emma's house, trying his best to exude a calm aloofness he didn't feel. At least not according to his heart, which beat like he'd run a marathon.

Abby sat in the seat next to him, a potted hydrangea in her lap, fidgeting with the hem of a short blue and white sundress. A sundress much like the style she'd worn when they dated. With its short length, it barely hit mid-thigh and revealed miles of long legs, ending with a pair of flip-flops because of her ankle injury.

How was he going to make it through the night without embarrassing himself with a hard-on? He'd been halfway there since picking her up.

"Thanks for bringing me this ankle brace," Abby said. "My mom was going to drop one off for me later, but you beat her to it."

"No problem. You'll still need to ice and elevate it a few times a day, but it will help stabilize it."

"Enough to climb a ladder?" she asked.

He cast her a sideways glance. "Not funny. Besides, with the painting done, there should be minimal ladder climbing necessary."

"We'll see," she said in a sweet tone he remembered meant she'd do whatever she damn well pleased.

Connor parked in the driveway of Emma and Jason's house. The seventy-five-year-old, four-bedroom, three-and-a-half-bath

Victorian home was dark gray and accented with pink trim. A wide set of stairs led up to a wraparound porch. A large picture window spanned the front of the right side of the house, with a bay window off one of the upstairs rooms.

It was a traditional home with a lot of history, which made it a wet dream for someone in the home renovation business. Jason had shared changes Emma wanted to make, and together the brothers kicked around a few ideas.

"This house is huge," Abby said.

"It was Emma's grandparents'. After her grandma passed away earlier this year, Emma's mom gave the house to her."

"Oh, right—I heard Anna is engaged to the mayor."

"They moved into John's house a few weeks ago."

"A house is some gift."

Connor turned off the truck and reached into the back seat for the pie he'd bought. He may have come from a dysfunctional family, but his mom had taught him to never show up empty-handed.

Moving quickly to the passenger side, he helped Abby down, his fingers grazing hers as he closed the door.

"Are you sure it's okay for me to be here?" Abby asked, her forehead furrowed with worry.

"I texted Emma, and she said the more the merrier."

Abby bit her lower lip. "I haven't been the nicest person to Emma or the Erickson family."

Connor recalled the protest Abby was part of a few weeks ago while they were filming *Beach House Flippers*. Emma's family struck a deal with the town council for a land swap that would have allowed them to expand Erickson Fun Pier in exchange for property next to their arcade. Once built and covered with rides, including the new roller coaster, the added portion of the pier would have blocked the beach view from the stores on the opposite side of the boardwalk. Abby's new business was one that would have been affected, and she, along with many others, had fought against the expansion.

"Because of the protest, we found a better solution that didn't involve taking up beach space or blocking views," Connor said.

"I know, but I should have voiced my concerns earlier. It wasn't like I didn't know about the plans. I just didn't realize the full impact until construction started."

"Don't be so hard on yourself. We all make mistakes."

"I'm the last person Emma and anyone in that house wants to see."

"It's all good. I promise." Without meaning to, he pressed a kiss to her forehead.

She flinched but quickly recovered, pressing into him and placing a warm hand on his waist.

What the hell had he been thinking? Abby hadn't given him any reason to think she was still into him. At least he hadn't kissed her lips, which he wanted to do more than he wanted air.

"Come, let's go." He stepped back and gestured for her to walk in front of him. "Emma said they'll be in the backyard."

He led her to the side of the house toward a white picket fence that separated Emma's property from Evan Carmichael's. Evan and Jason were best friends and had put Connor and Jason up when they first returned to Pelican Bay for the pier renovation.

The sound of summer beach tunes drifted through the air as they opened the gate. As they got closer, they caught sight of a little girl shrieking while running across the yard.

"That's Maddy's girl, Dylan. She's four and has all the adults wrapped around her little finger," Connor explained.

"Including you?"

Dylan shrieked even louder when she spotted Connor. "Uncle Connor, you came!"

The toddler ran full speed at Connor. He started to kneel, but between holding the pie and feeling a bit off his game with Abby next to him, he wasn't quick enough to prepare for the onslaught, and found himself flat on his ass.

Abby was speechless as Connor stumbled and fell when the girl launched herself at him before settling on his lap with her arms thrown around his neck.

"Hi, princess. How's my favorite girl?" Connor asked, not at all bothered at having been tackled to the ground by a child.

"I'll take that finger wrapping as a yes," Abby said with a laugh, and fought to push aside feelings she'd long ago buried.

Or so she thought.

Do not go there.

Dylan placed a wet kiss on Connor's cheek and turned to Abby. "Hi, I'm Dylan. Are you Uncle Connor's girlfriend? Are you staying for dinner? We're having burgers and hot dogs and pickles. I love pickles, do you?"

Abby's eyes widened at the speed at which the girl fired questions at her.

Then, before Abby could even answer, the bundle of energy took off.

"Wow, what happened?" Abby said. "I feel like I got hit by a wave and just came up to the surface."

Connor rose to his feet, dusting off his shorts. "Yeah, that's Dylan. She asks more questions than a murder investigator."

"Or so many questions you'll think you've committed a crime," Jason said, rounding the corner. "Hey, bro, Abby. Glad you could come."

"Thanks for having me," Abby said.

"Hope you're hungry. There's enough food for the entire block," Jason said.

They made their way behind the house, where two men stood on the patio in front of a massive grill. Beyond them was an enclosed porch and a spacious yard overlooking the bay.

"Hey, man," the tallest of the guys said, and did a handshake slash fist-bump thing with Connor.

"Hey, Ev. You remember Abby, right?" Connor said.

"Sure do." He offered his hand to shake.

"And this is Emma's brother, Tyler."

Another tall, good-looking guy, a few years younger with short, dark blond hair, offered a hand.

"Hi, Abby." Tyler turned, and she caught sight of a hearing aid in his left ear.

Although she'd never met him, Abby remembered he'd gotten injured when he tried saving Maddy during Hurricane Samantha. While Maddy suffered no physical injuries, Tyler had lost a portion of his hearing in one ear.

Connor held up the pie box. "We'll bring this inside."

Abby followed him inside the enclosed porch, which had a long table set for dinner. French doors led to the kitchen, where Emma and Maddy were mixing a frozen drink.

Emma had turned off the blender and poured the frozen concoction into a glass with a salted rim.

Maddy tasted it. "Perfection."

"Hey, Abby, Connor," Emma said, taking a step forward to hug Connor.

Abby stood awkwardly next to Connor, unsuccessfully trying not to feel like the odd one out. Most of the people here weren't family, but they'd been friends since their teenage years and likely knew everything about each other.

Why had she let Connor convince her to come?

"This is for you." Abby held out the purple and blue hydrangea.

"Thanks so much. It's beautiful, and will make a perfect centerpiece for the table." Emma accepted it and gave Abby a hug.

"Nice to see you, Abby. You like margaritas?" Maddy held a glass out to her.

"What's not to like?" Abby said.

There was a cry, and Dylan came tearing through the house into the kitchen with a puppy on her heels.

"Aunt Emma, Sandy keeps licking me," Dylan said.

"Because you keep teasing her with food," Maddy said, and picked up the toddler.

"Who is this little lady?" Connor bent down to pet the puppy, who was loving every minute of his attention.

"This is the newest member of the family," Emma said. "Meet Sandy."

Abby bent down and joined in rubbing the dog's belly. "A golden retriever, right?"

"Yes. Someone in town had puppies up for adoption, and Jace and I had been talking about getting one," Emma said.

"It's smart to get all the house breaking in before you renovate," Connor said.

"Jace said the same thing," Emma replied.

"Uncle Connor, can you come out and play with me and Sandy?" Dylan asked, wriggling to get out of her mother's arms.

"Sure, sweetheart. Let's go," Connor said with a wink to Abby.

Maddy set down Dylan, who chased Sandy out the door. "Abby, stay and hang in here with us."

Abby watched Connor trail after them. "She's going to terrorize that poor puppy."

"Most definitely," Maddy said.

"Here's to maybe five minutes of peace." Emma clinked glasses with the girls.

"How's the shop coming along?" Emma asked.

Abby sighed. "Renovations are slower than I hoped." She pointed down to her bandaged ankle. "I had a minor mishap yesterday."

"Oh no. What happened?" Maddy asked.

"I was running by the ocean and tripped. It's only a sprain, but there's a lot of work left to get ready for opening," Abby said.

"It's next week, if I remember," Emma said. "Need help? I'd be glad to pitch in."

"Me too," Maddy added.

Wasn't Natalie always busting her chops because Abby never felt comfortable asking for help?

"It's nice of you to offer, but I'm sure you both have your own stuff to do."

"It's not a problem," Emma replied.

"Besides, we're dying to get a preview of your products," Maddy said.

Maybe two more sets of hands plus more female perspectives would be useful.

"Sure. Thanks. Heads-up, things are a real mess," Abby said.

Outside, there was a crash followed by the bark of a puppy and Dylan shrieking.

Maddy and Emma exchanged a glance and rolled their eyes.

"Good thing we're used to working with chaos," Emma said, and drained her margarita glass.

Chapter Six

ABBY SLEPT THROUGH THE night with the help of two margaritas. Thanks to her internal clock, she'd woken without aid from an alarm a little past six a.m. Stretching in bed, she wished for the days when she could sleep as late as she wanted.

Rolling onto her side, she thought about last night. Dinner at Emma and Jason's had been surprising. Abby hadn't expected to fit in, but after her initial awkwardness, she realized there was no reason to worry.

The house had been full of noise and laughter. Dylan chased poor Sandy around the yard until they both dropped from exhaustion. After a round of flashlight tag with the guys, Tyler carried the sleeping toddler upstairs to bed, while the puppy passed out in a dog bed in the kitchen.

Abby was no stranger to a busy household, having grown up sharing a bedroom with two sisters and her nephew...at least until they moved to Pelican Bay.

The adults continued to hang out late into the evening, with Jason turning on the gas firepit for warmth in the cooler night air. String lights along the outside of the porch plus an assortment of lighted mason jars bathed the backyard in soft, romantic light.

Connor sat next to her in an Adirondack chair, sometimes touching her hand to get her attention and leaning close to give her insight to an inside joke. She expected—or perhaps hoped—he would make a move when he dropped her off, but he walked her upstairs, made sure she got in safely, and left.

Which left Abby restless, despite the two cocktails, and confused by her feelings for the man she'd convinced herself she was over.

Watching Connor with Dylan stirred thoughts Abby had long ago pushed aside. She stretched onto her back and covered her stomach with her hands, yearning for what had never been. She'd seen what her sister went through as a single mom. So, when Abby found herself pregnant at twenty, it was no surprise she had freaked out. Based on her calculation, it had happened around the night of Hurricane Samantha. By the time she missed her period and had taken the pregnancy test, Connor and his family had moved to Florida.

Although they had promised to stay in touch, they had made no long-term plans or commitment to each other.

Why would they when they were practically kids themselves, partying and not taking life seriously?

Seeing the blue lines on the stick had been a wake-up call to Abby. Not long after she had the results and had broken the news to her mom and sisters, she called Connor to let him know. She hadn't expected him to do anything, but it was the right thing to do.

He took it well, considering, and after the initial shock, promised to work hard and earn enough money to get back to New Jersey so they could be together when the baby was born.

A month later, Abby miscarried.

Now, all the feelings she'd worked hard to push aside were resurfacing. Would she have made a good mom? Would Connor have returned to Pelican Bay like he'd promised? Had the baby been a boy or a girl? Would they have still been together?

All questions without answers.

Rising from the bed, she went into the bathroom to shower. As usual, Abby did the only thing she could do. She pushed the feelings way down and got ready for a hard day of work.

Thirty minutes later, she sat on a stool at the worktable in the back of the shop, drinking a cup of coffee. Setting it down, she rummaged in a box of supplies. She'd been thinking a lot about what she and Nat talked about yesterday regarding giving out free soap samples. Emma and Maddy had encouraged her to do it, even promising to meet up with her and Natalie tonight to talk about the opening.

It took two trips of hunting through boxes to find what she needed to make the soap. She worked an hour straight, melting, mixing, and pouring the molds. She left them out on the counter to solidify and was cleaning up her tools when Natalie entered.

"Morning, sis," Natalie said. "Wow, you've been busy."

"The pros and cons of living above your business."

"This is for the samples, right?"

"Yes. I think we should do it," Abby said.

"Yay. I've warned Liam that if he doesn't get his ass together and show up to Harrison's for work, I'll put him to work here."

"Glad to know your parenting skill involves threatening your son and using our business as a type of community service."

"I'm at my wit's end with what to do with him. The kids he's hanging with are hellbent on finding trouble." Natalie poured herself a cup of coffee.

"Have you talked with his dad about it?"

"A little. Jake offered to have Liam move to Philly and live with him part time."

"Seriously? You said you'd never do that because Jake could barely take care of himself," Abby reminded her.

"He's met someone. Told me she's expecting, and they're getting married in September. He got a steady job and everything."

"Wouldn't a new wife and kid make Jake even less likely to pay attention to his son?"

"I guess...I don't know. You see how desperate I am?" Natalie exhaled a frustrated sigh.

Abby grabbed a towel and started drying her tools. "I think it's time to talk to Mom. She raised us, right? And we were no picnic."

"And look where it got her. One daughter pregnant at eighteen. Another wild and partying. No wonder Liam's a mess with us as role models."

"At least Livvie turned out okay," Abby said.

Their youngest sister had recently received her degree in physical therapy and gotten her first job. Hopefully, she'd learned from her two older sisters' mistakes.

Natalie jumped off the stool. "Enough of this depressing crap. Should we get back to painting?"

"Don't need to. It's done."

"How'd you manage that?"

Abby twirled the end of her ponytail. "Connor came by yesterday afternoon and helped me finish it."

"Do you own a jigsaw?"

Unless it was a puzzle, she had no clue what a jigsaw was or whether she needed it, but refused to respond.

"Or a level, or the molding and trim work to finish it nice?" He continued to come closer until Abby found her ass pressed against the worktable.

"I have a level," she replied, trying to ignore the warmth of his body, dangerously close to hers.

He captured her hands in his. "We have all the tools we need right here with us now. Give us a couple of days, and we can have your space functional. Then you can focus on stocking and getting ready for the opening."

She opened her mouth to argue, but he glanced over her shoulder to where the freshly poured soap molds sat. "You made these?"

"This morning. Nat and I talked about setting up a table and giving out samples."

"It's a good idea. While Jace, Ev, and I are out there working, you can be in here making more products and samples. It's a win-win, Abs."

"How's it a win for you?"

"Because I get to spend time with you." He tilted up her chin, forcing her to meet those glorious green eyes.

Their mouths were close, and the warmth of his breath brushed against her face. She wanted those lips on hers. All she had to do was reach her arms up and let it happen.

"Is that a yes, Abby?"

She should continue to fight, but her resolve had checked out. His points were valid, and who was she fooling? She and Nat could barely paint. If they tried to install flooring, who knew what damage they'd do?

"Yes, dammit. Next time, ask first." She pushed at his chest. "Now get to work."

He laughed and gave her a quick peck on the cheek. "You won't regret this, Abs."

When he reached the laminate flooring in a stack against the wall, he bent over, giving her a fine view of his perfect ass, grabbed a couple of boxes, and disappeared into the main room.

Abby raised a hand to touch her cheek, which tingled from where he'd kissed her. She might live to regret his help, but one thing was for sure...things were heating up between them.

And she was powerless to stop it.

Worse, she was no longer sure she wanted to.

Tonino's Pizza and Pasta had been a popular hangout on Pelican Bay for as long as Connor could remember. As soon as he was old enough to get working papers, Connor had applied for a job and started delivering food, either on foot or using one of the bicycles to carry pizza boxes and takeout bags. It was the perfect job because Mr. Tonino would give all the staff a free meal per shift and leftovers for them to take home.

Which often meant the difference between eating the next day or not.

Now the place was run by Mr. Tonino's sons, Mick and Steve. Mick was Connor's age and had been someone he used to party with. Steve was in Jason's grade. They had a younger sister, Nikki, who was closer to Tyler's age, and Kylie, who was somewhere in her early twenties.

From what Connor had observed the past few months, the changes Mick and Steve had made were paying off. They'd leased the lot next to them, doubling their space, and added a second story with a deck, providing an oceanfront view. Plus, they had a bar, jukebox, and stage area. Each day they rotated events, such as trivia and game night. With a stage, they brought in local bands and even had karaoke once a week. Now, the place was packed both with Pelican Bay natives and tourists—a sign that business was picking up.

Connor, Jason, Evan, and Tyler were regulars on Tuesday nights, since it was game night. They shot pool, threw darts, and even played poker when the mood struck.

Connor lined up his shot, pulled the stick back, and hit the cue ball into the stack of balls he'd racked up. The colored solid and striped balls scattered across the pool table, two of the striped balls sinking into pockets.

"He does it every time, man," Evan said before taking a swig of beer. "Takes the lead on the break."

"And cleans our asses up," Jason finished. "Tell me about it. I've had to deal with him my entire life."

Connor ignored them, lining up his next shot and pocketing two more before missing.

"You're jealous because it always got me the girls," Connor said.

"True dat," Jason said, and clinked beer bottles with him.

"Maybe you can share your tips," Evan said, lining up his own shot. "Jace is taken, and the well's been dry for me."

"You and me both," Connor said.

"Make that three of us," Tyler added, joining them.

Evan took his shot and missed. "In fact, your overall cheerfulness since you've been getting laid is downright annoying."

Connor and Tyler murmured their agreement.

Jason laughed. "Regular sex has definitely improved my quality of life."

Tyler winced. "Let's not talk about how you're sleeping with my sister. I live in the same house and don't need to think about what you two do down the hall from my bedroom."

"There's another pretty lady living in the same house," Jason said.

Tyler took the pool stick from Evan. "Dylan's a little young for my taste. Besides, I prefer someone who doesn't wear half her food on her face and doesn't smell like apple juice."

"What about Dylan's mommy?" Evan said. "She's a fairly neat eater, unless spaghetti is involved, and she looks and smells a lot better."

Connor smirked at the subtle-not-subtle way Evan was attempting to pump Tyler for information. It was impossible not to notice the sexual tension between them, but neither would admit to being into each other.

"Then why haven't you ever gone after her?" Tyler said, and lined up his shot.

"I made a move in high school," Evan said.

Tyler had just started to shoot but missed the cue ball completely. He tried to laugh it off, but Connor caught the flash of jealousy in his eyes before proceeding with his shot, which sank the cue ball.

He swore and turned the stick over to Jason.

"And?" he said to Evan. "What of it?"

Evan shrugged. "Was like kissing a sister. We swore to never speak of or do it again."

Tyler nodded in relief. "It didn't affect your friendship?"

"Nah. We joked about it for a while, but it's in the past," Evan said. "Besides, she's into you, man."

Tyler considered before shaking his head. "She's been staying at the house. I would know."

"It's true, bro," Jason added. "I've seen her watch you when you're not looking."

"Emma would kill me. She's her best friend."

Connor noticed Tyler hadn't denied having any interest.

"She wouldn't. Trust me," Jason said.

The loud rise of laughter came from the front near the bar as a group of girls came in, including Emma, Maddy, Jenna, Natalie, and Abby. The five of them took a large, round table and spread papers across it.

Connor noticed Ty's expression of yearning when he caught sight of Maddy. Yeah, there was definitely interest on his side, too.

"You should go for it," Connor added. "At least test the waters."

Tyler grabbed the empty bottles off the ledge. "I'll get this round," he said, and headed to the bar.

"A soda for me," Connor called after him. "That's an interesting group." He nodded at the table with the ladies.

"Emma said something about her and Maddy brainstorming ideas with Abby and Natalie for their business," Jason said.

"And you didn't stop them?" Connor said.

Jason snorted. "I just started getting some after my own dry spell. I'm no fool."

Poor Abby was going to be overwhelmed by Emma, who was known for her detailed planning and lists. During the renovation of Erickson Pier, she'd driven them all crazy with her lists, texting, and checking in with Jason and Connor two or three times a day.

"Hell, Emma took a laptop out of her bag," Connor said.

"Let's give them thirty minutes," Evan said with a smirk.

Connor had once prided himself on being the king of fun, but ever since getting unknowingly filmed while having sex with a former assistant on *Beach House Flippers*, he'd been walking the straight and narrow.

Maybe it was time for some fun.

"What do you have in mind?" he asked.

"We send them a round of shots," Evan said.

"That's all you've got?" Connor said. "No wonder you don't have a lady."

"You're one to talk." Evan gave him a light shove. "Sexily named shots we hand-deliver, and we pick the recipient."

Jason raised an eyebrow. "What, are you still in college?"

"Oh, come on. It will be fun," Evan returned.

Connor shrugged. "Go for it, man."

While the ladies worked, the guys finished their game of pool, and, as predicted, Connor cleaned house. When they were done, Evan headed to the bar to place the shot order.

Connor didn't know how Ev's plan would go over—and didn't care, if it meant more time with Abby. After spending the past two days at her shop, he realized that while they'd both changed, his feelings for her hadn't.

Maybe it was time to see if those feelings were reciprocated.

Chapter Seven

Abby had scribbled more than a page of notes when the server delivered the second pitcher of margaritas. She hadn't eaten since lunch, which explained the mild alcohol buzz. She grabbed another breadstick, pushing aside the pang of guilt from the additional carbs.

"When will Connor and Jace finish laying the floor?" Maddy asked.

"They should finish tomorrow," Jenna said. "Connor mentioned there's other work, like hanging light fixtures and assembling furniture, so I'd say two days max."

"Let's not forget the back area. It's a disorganized mess," Natalie piped up.

"We can help. You need an area for inventory, plus somewhere to store supplies used to make your products," Emma said.

"I'd also suggest an area to ship orders," Maddy added.

"Ship orders?" Abby asked. "Won't they be coming into the store to make their purchases?"

"Sure, in the beginning. What happens after summer is over and people from out of town return home?" Emma said.

"You want customers to keep buying your products even if they can't physically get to your store," Maddy added.

Abby had learned product marketing in college and should have thought about this, but she'd focused on getting the storefront open and hadn't considered offering options such as online purchases. Truth be told, there were so many things to think about as a business owner, it was easy to get overwhelmed.

"We created a website," Abby said. "But it needs help."

Maddy reached for Emma's laptop, brought up the site, and cringed. "I can work on this. I helped refresh the Erickson Pier website and can get an online store set up for you."

"There's a lot we haven't worked out yet," Natalie said.

"No worries. That's why we're here." Emma said.

"Why?" Abby asked before she could stop herself. "I was a bitch to you when I first moved back. I organized the protest to stop the Erickson Pier expansion. Why would you want to help me?"

"You raised valid points about the expansion," Emma said. "And with help from Jace, Connor, and their dad, we found a better way to handle the expansion than taking up beach space."

"But still…" Abby said.

Emma touched her forearm. "Really, Abby. No harm done. I promise. I consider you a friend and want to help."

The other ladies at the table all voiced their agreement.

Abby was touched at the ease with which they could forgive and forget.

"I can't tell you how much this means. I'm not good at asking for help," Abby said.

"That's what I've been trying to tell her," Natalie added.

"Why don't we come over tomorrow and see what needs to be done? It may seem overwhelming now, but it won't seem as bad with a few extra hands," Jenna said.

Although Abby wasn't as convinced, she nodded and let her friends refill her margarita glass. She needed to eat before all the alcohol went to her brain. Thankfully, her shop and apartment were a half a block down the boardwalk, and she could stumble home.

"What do you say we order food?" Abby said.

"Did someone say food?" Connor said, followed by a group of guys, including Jason and Tyler, all carrying pizza pies, and Evan carrying a tray of shots.

"I win," Emma said after a glance at her watch.

Abby wrinkled her brow. "Win what?"

Maddy groaned. "We had a bet on how long it would take for these clowns to crash our party." She dug in her purse and handed Emma a five-dollar bill. "I lost."

"At least they came bearing food," Jenna said.

"And drinks," Evan added. "All right, ladies, listen up. There's a special cocktail for each of you. Each of us will choose one, and you have to drink it, no questions asked."

Abby rolled her eyes. Someone was a little too enthusiastic about this game.

"I'll go first," Evan said. He selected a yellow shot and set it down in front of Jenna. "A flaming lemon drop for you, Jen."

She shrugged and tossed it back. "Mmm, that was good."

Evan passed the tray to Jason, who picked up a glass with a creamy-colored concoction. "A buttery nipple for you," he said, setting it in front of Emma.

Emma flushed and, after taking a tentative sip, downed the contents.

Tyler went next. After deliberating, he chose the darker-colored liquor and set it down in front of Maddy. "Alice in Wonderland seems appropriate."

"It's one of Dylan's favorite stories," Maddy said, and held Tyler's gaze as she chugged it down.

Evan had grabbed someone from the bar, since there were an uneven number of guys to girls. "Ethan's going to help us out."

"Hi, ladies." He scanned the table until landing on Natalie. He picked up the dark pink drink and handed it to her. "A Jolly Rancher, I believe."

After she downed it, only one shot remained.

Connor picked it up and smelled it before placing it in front of Abby. "An orgasm for you, Abs."

They all hooted and cheered her on as she picked up the creamy liquid. But their voices didn't matter. Abby focused all her attention on the man who had straddled a chair and watched her with dark green eyes.

She licked her lips and ran her tongue around the rim of the shot glass, which caused the group to holler even louder, before swallowing it in one gulp.

Connor threw back his head and laughed.

The guys brought over more chairs, and they ate until Abby thought she'd burst.

Music played on the jukebox, and after they'd eaten their fill, Connor held out a hand to her. "Let's dance."

Abby wiggled her foot. "Maybe not a wise move between my ankle and the alcohol."

"I'll make sure you don't fall."

She placed her hand in his and let him lead her to the dance area, trying to control her racing heart. The song playing was a slow, heartfelt Adele tune, and swaying to it while in Connor's arms transported her to a different time when they danced on the beach. Back then, they did whatever they wanted without worry or apologies.

They were different now...older...responsible.

All words Abby used to correlate with a boring and settled person.

But with the strength of Connor's arms surrounding her as they swayed, thoughts of being settled weren't even close to her mind. Memories of the past coursed through Abby, making her feel more like her teenage self than she had in years. Lighter, carefree, and a little reckless.

Perhaps it was the alcohol.

Or the man.

The rest of their friends joined them on the dance floor. Some, like Jason and Emma, danced and kissed. Others, like Evan and Jenna, moved with exaggerated turns and dips. Then there were Tyler and Maddy, who danced smoothly but with an awkwardness that made Abby wonder if they hated touching each other or were doing their best not to rip each other's clothes off.

Abby would bet on the latter.

Connor hummed to the music when he danced. She remembered he loved music and had taught himself guitar after finding one in the trash. Now, the vibration of his voice against her ear was an aphrodisiac sensation spreading through her body.

"Do you still play the guitar?" she asked.

"I do. Helps mellow me when I'm not able to sleep."

"You used to sleep half the day away," she teased.

His smile didn't reach his eyes. "It was the drugs. Without them, I had to find ways of occupying my mind. Playing music helps."

The more time Abby spent with Connor, the more she noticed the subtle ways he'd changed...matured. On the surface he looked the same, but now his eyes were clear and held a bit of sadness that had never been there before.

Perhaps she could take away some of the sadness. Tilting her head up, she pressed a light kiss to his lips.

Connor froze at the press of Abby's lips against his. They were warm and soft...familiar and yet not.

The old Connor would have devoured her. Rather, he held her tight, inhaling her sweet floral scent, and wanting to cherish the feel and taste of her. Even though it had been almost a decade since they'd touched like this, all the old feelings came crashing back to him.

Teaching her to surf...bonfires on the beach...swimming in the moonlight...making love.

Endless hours of making love.

Slowly, almost hesitantly, he sipped from her lips, small nips meant to arouse and seduce. And from the way Abby was pressing against him, as though she were trying to climb into his body, she was both.

Wanting her was no surprise. Abby had always been his kryptonite. He'd been with his share of women after moving to Florida. They each were nice, but he'd hoped to find a spark...something special to make him want more than one night or a few weeks.

Feelings he'd never experienced with anyone except Abby.

Even after everything they'd been through, their chemistry hadn't dimmed.

The enormity of it threatened to overwhelm him.

He broke away and whispered in her ear, "Let's walk on the beach."

She nodded, and he led her through the crowd, stopping so she could grab her bag and to let Jason know they were leaving.

Outside, he breathed in the warm air that held a hint of salt and dampness from the sea. He pulled Abby beside him and across the boardwalk until they descended the stairs, needing the feel of the cool sand on his feet.

Ever since rehab, he'd recognized the signs of when things overwhelmed him. In the past, he'd pop pills or smoke a joint to tamp it down. But he refused to give in to the temptation, even when the weight of everything seemed to press in on him.

"Slow down, Con. I can't keep up with my ankle," Abby said.

He slowed. "Sorry...I forgot."

He kicked off his shoes at the bottom of the stairs and waited while Abby slid out of her sandals.

Taking her hand again, he headed to the water. At the edge, he dipped his feet in, welcoming the splash of water against his legs.

A warm hand touched his shoulder. "What's wrong?" Abby asked.

"It was stuffy in there. Needed some fresh air."

"You forget how well I know you. Tell me what's got you freaking out."

He should have known it would be impossible to hide anything from her.

Backing away from the water's edge, he moved to where the sand was soft and sat, holding his hand up for her to join him.

She lowered herself beside him, raising the short length of her dress to an almost indecent length.

With her hand in his, he traced the pads of his fingers along the inside of her palm. "Being on Pelican Bay has brought back a lot of memories," he began.

"Understandably."

"Not all good memories."

She nudged his shoulder. "I remember many good memories."

A smile pulled at the corners of his lips. "I remember them, too. Mostly." He turned to face her. "I spent our entire relationship high on something."

"I did my fair share, too."

"You didn't crave it the way I did. It became a necessity to survive each day. Often needing it more than food...more than air."

"There was a lot going on in your life with your family."

He shook his head. "Jace went through the same shit. He didn't screw up his life like I did."

She moved closer and covered both his hands with hers. "You didn't screw up your life."

He snorted. "I came pretty damn close."

"Close doesn't matter. You're good now, right?"

He met her gaze. "I've been in recovery for eight years, nine months, and five days."

"You got the help you needed. That's what matters."

He mostly agreed with her, but sometimes it didn't seem to matter at all. Like now. Facing his past and his lack of responsibility was an important part of dealing with the addiction and stopping himself from getting bogged down in self-doubt and negative thoughts.

"I'm sorry, Abby."

She stiffened, getting his meaning without him needing to speak the words. But therapy had taught him saying the words was part of owning up to your mistakes and healing.

"I'm sorry about the baby...about our baby."

Abby snatched her hands away and played with the hem of her dress. "Let's not do this."

"Not talk about it? Why not?"

"Because I've put it behind me."

"Really? Because I sure as hell haven't."

He'd unlocked the lid to Pandora's box, and it was time to open it all the way.

"You shocked the hell out of me when you called to tell me you were pregnant."

"We weren't always careful."

"No, we weren't. And that's on me."

"It's on both of us."

He remembered the spontaneity of sex with Abby. She'd been adventurous, willing to try every crazy place and position he suggested. They couldn't keep their hands off each other, and condoms cost money he didn't always have.

"After the initial shock, I was happy. Freaked out because we lived a thousand plus miles away from each other, but happy because I loved you and the idea of starting a family with you."

"You said you would come back to Pelican Bay when you saved enough money," she said.

"And I meant it. Then I started thinking about what kind of father I'd be. Would I be an alcoholic and drug user like my dad? I already was more than halfway there with drugs. How would I support you and a child?"

"I never thought you'd be a bad father."

"I appreciate that. Worrying about it freaked me out, and I fell, Abby. Hard. I connected with some people in Tampa...bad people. I sold and used drugs. Experimented with hard stuff—cocaine—and landed in the hospital. I was forced into rehab for a couple of weeks. When I was released, I tried to stay clean. After a week, I fell into my old habits, and my mom and uncle put me back into rehab for forty-five days."

Connor wasn't ready to share the details of detoxing—the shaking...the tantrums...the nightmares...begging for a hit. It wasn't something he was proud of, but he'd gotten through it.

"That's where I was the time I called you." He gulped in a breath of air. "When you told me you had the miscarriage."

Until now, she'd held her composure, but he felt her tremble as tears trickled down her face.

"I'd gotten up in the middle of the night with cramps. When I went to use the bathroom, I saw the blood. I woke my mom to take me to the hospital, but it was too late." She hugged her sides and rocked back and forth.

He pulled her onto his lap, holding her as they both cried for the life they'd unknowingly created that had never gotten a chance.

"I'm sorry it happened...That I wasn't there for you."

"I know you are." She sniffled. "I saw how you were yesterday with Dylan. You were great with her."

"It was hard at first because I've often wondered if we would have had a boy or a girl. But it was easy to be comfortable with Dyl. I see a different world through her eyes. A world with wonder and possibilities."

"The way life should be at her age." She paused for a beat. "You'll be a good dad, Con."

"I hope to be one day." He hesitated before he asked the next question for fear of the answer. "Are you able to get pregnant again?"

She nodded. "The doctors told me the fetus wasn't viable, which is why my body rejected it. I can conceive again, and there's no reason to think I'd be at a higher risk to miscarry."

He leaned his forehead against hers. "I'm glad." He wiped away her tears. "So glad."

The half-moon offered faint light, and his lips met hers in a tender kiss.

"I know this was hard to talk about, but it's been on my mind since coming back," he said.

"Mine too. So, what do we do now?"

"What do you want to do? Can we move beyond the past?"

"I think we just did." She turned and straddled him. "What do you say to a redo?"

Chapter Eight

ABBY ARCHED HER HIPS, and the bulge she straddled grew thicker beneath her. Connor met her thrusts, his breath getting faster the harder he grew.

"A redo?" he asked.

"Why not? We've both changed...grown up."

And from the feel of what was between her thighs, he was bigger...everywhere.

She thrust her fingers into his shaggy, dark blond hair and kissed him. No hesitant kiss this time. She was certain she wanted him in her life.

Did he feel the same way?

He growled and opened his mouth to kiss her, his tongue hot and wild as it intertwined with hers in a desperate duel for more. Rough hands slid under the hem of her dress, and he lifted it enough to cup her exposed cheeks.

"I've been fantasizing about you in a thong," he said, his voice gruff and sexy. "It's all I've been able to think about since yesterday."

"Then it's a good thing I wore one."

When his fingers made their way to the front and swiped across her clit, she shuddered. "Keep going, Con."

He slid a finger under the elastic and stroked her. "You're soaked, darlin'."

She wanted to answer, but then he slid two fingers between her slick folds, and she gave in to the tension building in her. She moaned and moved against him, urging him to go faster...needing more.

With his fingers buried deep inside her, she captured his mouth until, with a final press on her clit, she cried out and fell apart in his arms.

"You take my breath away when you come." He trailed open-mouthed kisses down her neck, tugging the neckline of her dress down past her breasts.

She sucked in a breath when he slid a hand beneath the lace and cupped her breast before pulling the scrap of lace away. When he captured her nipple between his lips, her body started to climb again.

But this time wasn't only about her.

"Wait, Con."

He raised his head. "I'm sorry. Too fast, right?"

She shook her head and climbed off him. "Not fast enough."

Then she reached under her dress, yanked off the thong, and tossed it in his lap. Feeling like the carefree girl she'd once been—one who wasn't afraid to take chances—she gave him a saucy smile and walked backward into the water.

She waded out until she was waist deep and dipped under to get her entire body wet. When she surfaced, Connor sat frozen in the same spot.

She curled a finger, gesturing for him to join her. He blinked twice before he shimmied out of his shorts and shirt and charged into the water.

The laugh bubbled out of her as he caught her around the waist, making her feel younger and freer than she had in years.

Ocean-sprayed strands of hair fell across his face in a sexy shag.

He kissed her long and hard, his hands busy under her dress. She pushed at his boxer briefs, freeing his cock and causing him to groan while he pressed into her hand.

Thankful that the water was relatively calm, she wrapped her legs around his back and guided him inside.

"Dear God, Abby," he murmured as he thrust up, filling her. "You're killing me."

Tilting her pelvis, she pulled back before sinking back down on him.

"Don't have a condom," he said.

Powerless to stop, she kept moving, taking him in deeper with each thrust.

He slowed down and held her face. "Abby, I don't have a condom on."

She gulped in air. "I'm on the pill, and I'm clean."

"I'm clean, too." He pushed her hair out of her eyes. "You're sure about this?"

"I'm sure, Con. Make love to me. Here. Now."

He swore and kissed her, his hands moving to her hips and setting a mind-crippling pace. Abby kept up, her legs shaking with the exertion. He reached between them and stroked her, and she shattered, taking him along with her.

They held each other until the gentle sway of the water pulled them in toward shore. She wrung out her dress the best she could while Connor dragged on his shorts, slipped her thong into his pocket, and swept her into his arms.

She laughed. "What are you doing?"

He started toward the boardwalk. "Carrying you. You're going to need energy when we get to your place...and do this again."

She hugged him tight all the way to her apartment, where he made good on that promise and made love to her until they both fell asleep a little before sunrise.

Connor entered MBR using the back door, hoping he could slip upstairs and grab a quick shower before the morning meeting. His clothes were still damp and wrinkled due to them lying in a pile on the floor all night. But Connor was still riding the high from his night with Abby too much to care what anyone thought.

"Look who's doing the walk of shame," Jason said, leaning against the counter with a cup of coffee.

"No shame here," Connor deadpanned.

Definitely no shame. Not the first time he and Abby made love in the ocean. Nor the second as they showered off the sand and sea. Nor the third less than an hour ago before he left.

Jason studied him. "I can see."

"Going to grab a shower. Be down in ten."

As Connor passed Jason to get to the stairs, his brother reached out and put a hand on his forearm. "You know what you're doing, right, bro?"

After getting out of rehab, Connor looked at each day with a new appreciation. Determined to get his life on track, he worked hard and liked the fame that came from co-starring on a hit reality TV show. People recognized him when he went out, and it wasn't because he was that poor kid. Strangers recognized him for his accomplishments and the success of the show, which helped build up his confidence.

However, after the incident with the unintended sex post, Connor had lost faith in people and his own judgment. Almost a year later, he still avoided any entanglements.

Now, he spent his free time meditating, doing yoga, surfing, and playing his guitar, which helped him think about what he wanted long term. He wanted more than a one-night stand with someone who only wanted to say she fucked a celebrity.

Been there, done that. Not going back.

Connor wanted to feel alive and whole with someone who cared about him...someone he could build a future with. Last night with Abby had gone a long way to helping him achieve both.

"I know what I'm doing," Connor said.

"Okay." Jason relaxed his grip. "If something changes and you need an ear, you know I'm there for you. Anytime. Anywhere."

As one of the three people who knew what it was like to grow up in the Maguire household, his brother would always watch out for him. One hundred percent. They'd stuck together through thick and thin. Through drunken fights with their father, having to ask the neighbors for a couple of eggs so they'd have dinner, Connor's drug addiction, flipping their first house, celebrating their contract for *Beach House Flippers*, starting their business on Pelican Bay. No matter what, they had each other's backs.

"I know, bro. Thanks."

"I'll have another coffee ready when you get down."

Connor nodded and jogged up the stairs.

Twelve minutes later, he entered the conference room, notebook in hand. "Where are Jenna and Ev?"

"Seems everyone is off to a late start today," Jason muttered.

"Someone's cranky this morning," Jenna said, sauntering in and dropping a Shore to Please bakery box on the table and heading toward the kitchen.

"I'm not cranky," Jason called after her.

Connor pounced on the box, in dire need of calories to restore the energy he'd spent during his night with Abby.

Evan entered the conference room, a chipper smile on his face despite the early hour. "Morning."

"Who are you?" Jason asked. "Usually, you're half-asleep when we drag your ass in here before nine."

"Maybe I'm getting used to your crazy hours. And what's with you? You didn't get any last night?"

Jenna walked in with two mugs of coffee. Connor caught the flush in her cheeks and the slight linger of hands as she handed Evan a mug.

Perhaps Evan's streak of celibacy had also been broken last night. *Good for him.*

"Let's get started," Jason said. "I got a call early this morning about more vandalism at one of our properties."

"What the hell," Connor said. "Which?"

"The museum."

"We haven't started any work there except marking out the space," Connor continued.

"Thankfully, they couldn't do much more than childish pranks with silly signs and trash. Can you stop by there this morning, Con? We're starting renovations on the mini-golf site this morning, and I need to be there," Jason said.

"Sure, no problem. I'll go before I head over to Abby's. Need a couple hours to finish the floor before the furniture can be put in place," Connor said.

"This vandalism is becoming a problem," Evan said. "It started with the break-in during the Erickson Pier reno, then the mini-golf, and now this."

"I talked with Ethan about that last night. It's not only our properties. There's been a couple of incidents at Harrison's and a few other places," Jason said.

"Spreading the love," Connor said. "Stupid-ass punks."

"Do the cops have a suspect?" Jenna said.

"Maybe, but Ethan can't tell us who," Jason said.

"You think we should install cameras like we did at the pier?" Connor asked.

"May be a good idea," Jason said.

"Tell me what you need, and I'll take care of it," Jenna added, making notes on her iPad.

"Will do," Jason said.

"In other business, I should have a decent draft of the Dunes property by the end of the day," Evan said.

The Dunes was what they'd named the area they were going to renovate in their old neighborhood. Hurricane Samantha had ravaged the entire area, and it needed a serious overhaul. They'd kicked around several possibilities, and Evan, as their contracted-out architect, was putting together a couple of options.

"Perfect. Let's review them at tomorrow morning's meeting," Jason said. "Assuming we start on time."

"Do you hear something, Ev? I hear an annoying sound," Connor said, rising and grabbing another donut.

"I hear it too, but can't make it out," Evan agreed.

They all laughed and headed their separate ways.

Jason caught up with him. "You want to meet up here at six, before driving over to Dad's place?"

Connor had forgotten today was the day he and Jason had dinner at their dad's apartment. Since reuniting with him a couple of months ago, after his release from prison, they'd started weekly dinners to work on their relationship.

Not the most exciting of nights, but they'd promised their mom, who'd been traveling back and forth from Tampa, that they'd put forth the effort. Surprisingly, Allen Maguire had been true to his word and appeared to be clean and sober.

"Sounds like a plan," Connor said.

After grabbing a few things from his apartment, Connor texted Abby an approximate time he'd be at her shop, and drove to the lighthouse.

Five minutes later, he pulled into the parking area. The lighthouse area didn't draw the tourist crowd like it once did. The idea of building a museum had been Jason's. Emma had paintings and photographs she'd done over the past decade. Plus, old pictures she found in the attic of her house. Those, along with other things she was gathering from townspeople, would be displayed to share the history of the town. Combined with the nature trail and enhanced picnic area, it would provide a nice tourist stop.

Connor grabbed a trash bag and pair of work gloves from the bed of the truck and headed to the future site of the museum and nature trail. Trash littered the area that only yesterday he'd marked off with painting spray and string. Now, the string and the sticks lay broken, as though someone had run over them with a bike.

What kind of person thought so little to do this on town property? And was it connected to the other vandalism?

Connor frowned at the words spray-painted in fluorescent orange.

GO HOME

That exact phrase had been painted in several spots on Erickson Pier and also at mini-golf. No points for creativity.

Connor took a few pictures before picking up the trash. About halfway through, he caught a flash of something against the sunlight. Bending down, he picked up a necklace half buried in the rubble. A cheap stainless-steel chain with a baseball with the Philadelphia Phillies' *P* on it.

He and Jason had been all over this area multiple times and never seen this. Could one vandal be a kid?

Connor placed the chain in a pocket of his cargo shorts. He'd mention it to Jason later tonight, and they could give it to Ethan. It may not mean anything, but if it could help them find whoever was responsible for the vandalism, Connor was all for it.

Chapter Nine

RATHER THAN GRABBING A couple hours of sleep like she wanted to, Abby had risen after she kissed Connor goodbye. Now, freshly showered and dressed, she stood in front of the coffee maker as the first drops fell into her mug. Once it reached about three-quarters of the way full, she swapped out the mug with the pot, grateful for the sneak-a-cup feature. She added creamer and sugar and took a greedy sip. It was going to be the first of many cups she'd need today.

The view of the bed caught her eye, with its sheets rumpled from an early-morning round of sex.

Marvelous sex with Connor.

She could barely believe it had happened. After taking another mouthful of caffeine, she picked up her damp dress from the chair where she'd dumped it when she and Connor returned last night. She'd barely had time to remove it before he was dragging her into the shower, all hard and ready to go again.

There were notable differences in Connor. The obvious, of course, was that he wasn't using. He'd also only drunk one beer, changing over to soda or water even when everyone around him was drinking shots and second and third rounds of beers.

Then there were the physical changes. Younger Connor was thin...too thin. She knew it bothered him, which was why he'd worn baggy shirts. Whenever she could, she'd bring him leftovers from her house, because it was rare for him to eat three full meals a day.

Now he was all lean muscle, backed with bulk he hadn't had in his younger years. And while he still had a flat stomach, it wasn't from lack of eating. His ripped six-pack was rock hard and sexy as hell. Even his thighs had filled out, powerful as he held her when they made love in the ocean...and in the shower.

Just thinking about it got her hot for him again, and she busied herself changing the sheets on the bed.

But it was more than the sex. While he'd always been quick to laugh and make jokes, he now had focus...purpose. He took his job seriously and worked hard. She'd seen him when he was working on the Erickson Pier renovation. At first, she thought it was all fluff because he and Jason co-hosted *Beach House Flippers*. She'd assumed they read off the cue cards and, when the cameras were turned off, let the teams do the work.

She'd been wrong.

They banged, nailed, sawed, and did whatever was needed to get the job done. Both on and off camera. They directed the team, advised, and chipped in. And when that work was done, they did more.

Now, they'd set up shop on Pelican Bay and bought several properties on the island to renovate. Smart move on their part. There was plenty more to snatch up, too. For Sale signs could be seen everywhere. Truth be told, the town needed businesses like theirs, that could front the cost of the renovation and sell at a reasonable price, to draw people to the island.

Connor had gotten his shit together.

Unlike her.

Which was why Soap Sisters needed to be a success.

She finished making the bed and straightening up the room before heading downstairs, coffee carafe in hand. She'd made a full pot, enough for Natalie, and assuming Emma, Maddy, and Jenna were coming over like they'd planned yesterday.

They'd all had a good amount to drink last night between the margaritas and shots. Abby had stopped drinking earlier than all of them, and her midnight swim plus multiple orgasms at the hands of Connor left her tired but not hungover.

The door opened, and Natalie came in carrying a huge purse and a bag of bagels, with Emma and Maddy lagging behind her.

Emma walked slowly, without her usual pep, and although Maddy wore sunglasses, it did nothing to hide her pale complexion.

Maddy dragged herself onto a stool at the worktable and lowered her head onto her arms.

"Rough morning, ladies?" Abby said.

Emma grunted and held her head. Maddy moaned from beneath her arms.

"I'll take that as a yes," Abby said. "Coffee or something cold?"

"Coffee," Emma said.

Maddy kept her head down but put a thumb up.

"I'll get the aspirin," Natalie said.

Abby placed mugs in front of them and set another out for Natalie. "You didn't have to come over."

"We promised. We'll be okay," Emma said.

"Easy for you to say," Maddy said before reaching for the cream and sugar and drinking the coffee like a lifeline.

"How come you're not hungover?" Abby asked Natalie, who handed out aspirin and water.

"I drank water and left before the others," Natalie said.

"You both left early," Emma accused. "Abby slipped out with Connor and Nat with Ethan."

Abby raised her eyebrow. "You and Ethan?"

"It's casual...nothing serious," Natalie said. "And what's up with you and Connor? He's been spending a lot of time here the past couple of days."

"You know he's been helping get the store ready," Abby said.

"I think he's helping in other areas, too." Natalie walked over to the staircase and held up the black lace bra Abby had been wearing last night. She remembered Connor had removed it with his teeth while pinning her to the wall last night.

"Oh my God, you're blushing," Emma said.

Abby snatched the bra from Natalie and stuffed it in a drawer. "Okay, fine. He spent the night."

"I figured, the way you two were steaming up the dance floor last night," Emma said.

"Everyone in this room had sex last night except me. I hate you all." Maddy opened the bag and grabbed an onion bagel.

"Sorry?" Natalie said.

"I only dream of sex, which means I'm living vicariously through all of you." Maddy added a generous helping of cream cheese to the bagel. "Remind me how good it is again."

Abby laughed. "If you need to be reminded, then it's been too long."

"Try over four years too long." Maddy bit into her bagel.

"Four years?" Natalie and Abby said at the same time.

"*Over* four years," Maddy repeated. "The last guy I slept with was Dylan's dad. I did have a fantastic dream last night, though. I was outside on your patio, Em. Sitting in the chaise lounge by the firepit and kissing someone."

"Who?" Emma asked.

Maddy shrugged. "It was too dark to tell, but boy could he kiss. And his hands were pretty fine, too."

"Too bad it was a dream," Abby said.

"Tell me about it. But it means I have no reservations about eating all the carbs I want," Maddy said with a laugh, pausing midway to wince and put a hand to her head. "Remind me never to mix shots and margaritas."

"Same goes," Emma said. Setting down her cup, she cut a cinnamon raisin bagel in half. "I need to work to forget about my head. Tell us how we can help you."

"I think we should put together the shelves so we can unbox our stock and supplies," Natalie said.

Abby gestured at the stacks of boxes. "Somewhere in this mess are small bags. If we can find them, we can wrap the sample soaps I made yesterday."

"What if you printed coupons giving people ten percent off a purchase of twenty-five dollars or more and placed them in the bag with the samples?" Maddy said.

"Good idea. Can we print them ourselves?" Abby asked.

"You have a printer?" Maddy said.

Abby pointed to the desk in the corner. "It's still in the box."

Maddy refilled her coffee and grabbed her laptop. "Okay, I'm on tech."

Despite hangovers, the four of them worked all morning, assembling five freestanding shelves and loading them with supplies and products. They placed one in an area designated to pack orders for pickup or delivery. Abby made a list of shipping materials to purchase, plus other items such as gift baskets and tissue paper.

A little after noon there was a knock at the back door, and Jenna poked her head through. "Lunch delivery."

Connor trailed behind Jenna, who carried a large takeout bag. "Afternoon, ladies. Looks like I arrived at the right time."

"Connor has a knack for arriving on time when a free meal is involved," Emma said. "It's gotten to where I automatically set an extra place for him at dinner."

"Guilty as charged, and good to know," Connor said. "What Em here neglects to mention is that the food is payment for hours of late-night reno, like steaming off wallpaper."

"Sounds like bribery to me," Natalie said.

"I can live with that," he said.

Abby's pulse increased at seeing him, and she wasn't sure how to act, especially with her friends there. She'd been sitting on a stool at the worktable assembling a gift basket of products they were going to raffle off when people signed up for their online newsletter—which she technically didn't even have yet.

Connor helped take the decision out of her hands when he came over to her. "Hey, darlin'. You've all been busy."

"We've unpacked all my boxes and are wrapping soap samples to hand out," Abby said.

"Speaking of samples, here." Jenna opened her large tote bag and pulled out an assortment of printer labels.

"I'll take them," Maddy called.

She'd set up the printer on a box on the floor next to Abby's desk and was operating two laptops.

"This afternoon, we're going to set up a table outside the front of the store," Abby explained. "Maddy printed coupons to include with the samples."

"Smart idea," Connor said. "I'll work on finishing the front room. Anything you need me to do first?"

"As a matter of fact, yes. Follow me," Abby said, and led him into the shop area, where a large box that had been delivered late yesterday was lying.

"What is it?"

"The awning for the front of the store. Would you be able to hang it?"

"Sure, I'll do it now so it will be up before you hand out samples," he said. "But first…"

He slid his hands along her waist and pulled her close. "Hi." He kissed her, a slow, drawn-out kiss, like he had been waiting his entire life to kiss her despite having had his mouth all over her body only hours ago.

"Hi." She wrapped her arms around his neck and pressed against him, wishing they were alone and she could drag Connor onto the worktable.

He broke the kiss, but continued to hold her close. "Sorry I got here later than expected. Had to handle an issue at the lighthouse."

"What happened?"

"Someone decided it would be fun to mess with the area where the museum will be built."

"Oh no. How terrible. What'd they do?"

"Nothing major. Trash everywhere, ripped out the stakes we had used to mark the location, spray-painted signs."

"Seems to be a recurring theme around here."

"We're going to set up a couple of security cameras at all our properties and hope it helps Ethan and the police catch whoever is responsible."

"Makes sense," she said.

The sound of laughter came from the back room.

"I guess I should get started," he said, kissing her again.

"What are you doing tonight?"

"I have plans with Jace and my dad for dinner, but I can come over after if you're free."

"How about I pick up dessert?"

"Darlin', you *are* the dessert."

Abby laughed as he gave her another hot kiss before getting to work.

Dinner had taken longer than Connor hoped. His dad barbecued ribs and served them with ears of fresh corn and a medley of roasted vegetables. Neither Connor nor Jace cooked that often. Sure, they could manage, but their schedule kept them busy. Now, the brothers helped with the dishes.

Every week his dad cooked something different—a positive sign he was adapting to post-prison life. Besides his job at a garage in Sunset Bay—a town next to Pelican Bay—he attended daily AA meetings.

Although Connor had never had an issue with alcohol, he'd attended a few sessions with his dad to offer support. While there were similarities, Connor attended weekly Narcotics Anonymous meetings instead. He remembered the struggle and never took his long-term recovery for granted.

During the Erickson Pier renovation, his dad had been a lifesaver, volunteering many hours after his shift ended to lead the effort to restore the vintage carousel. Allen Maguire had a knack for anything mechanical and a little electrical. Growing up, when he lost his job as a mechanic, rather than find a new one, he turned to placing bets at the racetrack and drinking, which resulted in him losing all their money. And when his mom tried to compensate by working three jobs, rather than being grateful, his dad would come home in a drunken rage and pick fights with his wife—and his sons, too.

Connor had tried to help pay the bills by selling drugs because his father pressured him to. What made it even worse was that the money Connor earned wasn't used to pay for food and rent. Unfortunately, his dad would take Connor's earnings to the track, where he lost more than he won.

After Mrs. Erickson, Emma's late grandmother and former Pelican Bay mayor, had snagged him and Jason shoplifting from Harrison's Market, she helped them find jobs—a newspaper route for Connor and a groundskeeping position at the lighthouse for Jason. Once Connor turned sixteen, he'd been able to get the delivery job at Tonino's with a recommendation from Mrs. Erickson.

With her help, the boys had gotten on a right path—of sorts. Jace was fine, but Connor had walked the fine line with trouble. It all came tumbling down in Tampa, and he had thanked God that his uncle didn't give up on him, and forced him to get help.

Now, Connor had a new appreciation of life and spent every day being grateful to have gotten his shit together.

While his dad seemed to have put his past behind him, Connor couldn't help but wonder if his father would revert to his drinking ways. Jason shared the same concern, especially since their mom flew up from Florida every couple of weeks and was attending marriage counseling with their dad.

Initially, Jace and Connor had agreed to the weekly dinners to make sure their dad was staying true to his word. Things had changed over the course of the past couple months, and while Connor didn't look forward to their dinners, he didn't dread them as much as he had in the beginning.

Except tonight, when he was eager to see Abby.

"Great dinner, Dad," Jason said. "What'd you use to season the ribs?"

"It's a special rub I made. I'll write down the list of ingredients, if you'd like."

"I would. Thanks," Jason said.

Their dad fixed a pot of coffee and turned to them. "I'd like to talk with you both about something."

Connor glanced at Jason, who shrugged.

"What's up?" Connor asked, setting cream and sugar on the table.

"It's about your mom." He rubbed his hands on his legs a few times in a nervous habit. "I love her, and by some miracle, she still loves me. I want to marry her."

"Unless I've missed something, you're already married," Jason said.

"Legally, but your mom and I haven't been husband and wife in a long time."

"You don't need to be married for *that*, Pop," Connor said.

His dad flushed. "I don't mean like *that*. I mean living together, sharing a life together."

"What are you saying, Dad?" Jason asked.

"I want to ask your mom to remarry me, renew our vows, or whatever you want to call it. I want your blessing first."

"Our blessing? Why?" Connor said.

"Because you were there for her when I wasn't. You helped her through the worst time of her life. I won't move forward trying to rebuild a life with her if you both don't want me to."

"You're not the only one who's changed. Mom's stronger than she was," Connor said.

"If she wants to be part of your life, we can't stop her," Jason added.

"I know, but I'll walk away from her, and you, if it's what you both want."

Connor knew what their dad wanted. Forgiveness.

Could he and Jace give it to him?

"Where would you live?" Jason said.

"Tammy wants to move back here to Jersey. To be near me and both of you. She's going to rent an apartment for six months. Hopefully by then, my parole will be done, and we can remarry and move in together."

"How do you plan on rebuilding a life with her?" Connor asked. "Mom is used to a certain quality of life now."

"A life the three of us worked hard to make together," Jason added.

Their dad nodded, as if he'd been prepared for that question. "Besides working at the garage, I've started a side business making furniture. Outdoor furniture like Adirondack chairs, custom picnic tables. Also, indoor furniture like bookcases, desks, tables, and the like."

"When do you do that?" Jason asked.

"I have a lot of free time on my hands now that the pier renovation is done," He continued. "One of the guys who helped with the carousel renovation is working with me. We're renting out a shed on the garage property. It's a piece-of-shit space, but the owner is renting it to us for dirt cheap. We've made a few things and through word of mouth have gotten some custom orders."

Natalie headed to the front room and turned on the lights. "Wow, it turned out great. Maybe he can do the rest."

"I'm sure he has better things to do than help us."

"Maybe not, Abs. You should get out here."

Abby set down her towel and joined her sister in the front room. Natalie opened the front door, letting Connor, Jason, and Evan in carrying toolboxes and dressed in MBR shirts with work boots.

"What are you all doing here?" Abby asked, her eyes panning to Connor.

He gave her an easy smile that never failed to make her knees weak. "We're here to install your new floor."

While part of her wanted to jump at his offer, she was worried about becoming too accustomed to being around him and leaning on him for help.

Something she'd promised herself never to do again.

"Can I talk to you for a moment?" she asked him.

Without waiting for an answer, she led the way to the back room. Even though it hurt her ankle, she paced in long, angry strides.

He strolled in, sans the toolbox. "Let's not fight about this, Abby."

She stopped in front of him and crossed her arms over her chest. "You had intentions of coming here today all along and never once thought to ask me last night."

"Because I didn't want you to do what you're doing right now." He stepped forward, and the clean smell of him was enough to make her want to forget their past and pull him close.

"Natalie and I can handle this."

"Really?" He nodded at the piles of long boxes stacked on the floor. "You've installed a laminate floor before?"

"I've watched YouTube videos. How hard can it be?"

"You have any pictures?" Connor said.

Picking up his cell phone, his dad scrolled through his photo app. "Here's what we've made so far."

Connor and Jason studied the images. The quality of what they'd built was clear. Clean lines, sturdy wood.

"These look terrific," Connor said. "I'd think these would sell big around here."

"We're always scouting out this type of stuff during our renovations," Jason said. "Hell, Emma was just saying she wants to get new furniture for the patio and sunroom once we renovate them."

"I'm not asking for your help to sell them. I have a plan to support your mom and am not expecting her to support me."

"We're glad to hear it, Pop," Connor said.

"Does Mom know about this business?" Jason said.

"She encouraged me to do it." He paused and studied his lap. "She raised you fine boys, working three jobs she hated when I couldn't hold down one. And now, with her real estate license, she's really found something she loves. I'm proud of her and you. You were better off without me in your life."

Connor exchanged a glance with Jason, who nodded. "I had my share of screw-ups. My life could have gone a completely different way if Mom and Uncle Tom hadn't forced me into rehab. And I still fucked it up the first time. But family sticks together to support each other. Through good times and bad. Isn't that what they say during wedding vows?"

"The important thing is you've gotten help and are working on your relationship with Mom," Jace added.

"And us," Connor said.

Their dad nodded and wiped at his eyes. "She never gave up on me, and I don't know why not. I gave her more than enough reasons to."

"She never stopped loving you," Jason said. "Love is powerful. I didn't understand it before, but after finding Emma again, I get it. Relationships are a partnership."

"You're right. I promise both of you I will never be the man I was before. I want to be a father you're proud of." He didn't even try to wipe away the tears as they slid down his cheeks.

Connor placed a hand over his dad's, so much like his own. "We're proud you got help and are staying clean. I know how hard that is. We support you in continuing to stay clean."

Jason added his hand. "Including giving you our blessing to remarry Mom, if that's what she wants."

Their dad failed to stifle a sob. "Thanks. Means more than I can say. I love you both."

Neither Connor nor Jace could return the words, but they each put an arm around their dad in an awkward man-hug.

"I'll pour the coffee. Then maybe you can show us the workspace. I know a couple of guys who can patch things up, if you need it," Connor said.

Despite their past and his dad's flaws, he was trying to make amends.

Connor considered his history with Abby. He'd thrown away something good. When she'd gotten pregnant and needed him the most, rather than work hard and return to Pelican Bay like he'd promised her, he got tossed in jail and rehab. Not very different from his dad. By then, it was too late.

He regretted how he behaved and could think of many ways he could have handled things better. But the past couldn't be undone...The present and what lay ahead were what mattered now. Those were the things he could change, and he'd work hard to make the right decisions.

Strength and resilience gave you the tools to be a better person. Possibilities gave you hope for a better day...and a chance at a wonderful tomorrow.

He loved Abby. Always had.

It was time to put his heart on the line and tell her how he felt. Now was a chance for a new start.

Chapter Ten

AFTER RETURNING TO HIS apartment to get his truck and an overnight bag, Connor drove to Abby's. Lights from Erickson Pier lit up the sky, and the faint sound of laughter as a family walked home drifted through his open windows. The dad held a sleeping toddler in his arms, her arms clutching a stuffed unicorn Connor had seen at one of the game booths. The mom pushed a younger child in a stroller. They paused at a red light, and the dad put an arm around his wife and kissed her. A tender kiss that held the promise of a night and a lifetime of love.

Connor wanted that.

The wife...the children...a family of his own.

With Abby.

Would she want the same thing?

He parked in a resident-reserved spot in the lot behind Abby's building and turned off the engine.

Only one way to find out.

He grabbed his duffel bag and walked up the outside stairs that led to the apartment.

She answered wearing a loose-fitting dress, her hair damp and wavy, as though she'd just showered.

His heart raced as she smiled at him.

"Perfect timing. I read your text and took dessert out of the freezer," she said.

Stepping inside, he dropped his bag on the floor and spun her in a circle before kissing her. "You're all the dessert I need."

She laughed and wriggled out of his arms to close the door. "I have chocolate marshmallow ice cream."

He backed her against the door, already hard and wanting her more than his favorite ice cream. "Let's save it for later."

He slid his hands under her dress, groaning when he didn't encounter any barrier. Only skin. Soft skin pressed against him as he gripped her backside before sliding to the front, where he slid fingers along the rim of her clitoris before dipping in and finding her sleek and wet.

"I need you, Abby," he whispered, aware of how desperate he sounded, but beyond caring. He walked with her to the island and set her on top, pulling the dress over her head.

Fully naked underneath.

Sexiest sight ever.

"I approve of your choice of undergarments," he said, taking in her full breasts, which rose and fell like she'd been running.

"Now let's remove yours."

She yanked off his shirt while he shoved down his shorts and briefs in one swift move, kicking off his shoes along the way.

She had parted her legs and was reaching for him, but he had other ideas.

He bent down and traced his nose along her legs, taking in the floral scent of her body lotion—probably one of her own creations. When he reached her vagina, he inhaled the sweet scent of desire he could see glistening there. He blew gently, and her hands clamped into his hair, nudging him forward.

She cried out when he licked her. A slow, deliberate sip, as if he was tasting the most delectable dessert. And to him, she was a perfect combination of every dessert he'd ever had.

He sampled, going deeper with each thrust of his tongue, the press of her thighs against his face. When she trembled, he inserted a finger and sucked on her clit, and she pressed his head against her as she thrust her hips and cried out her release.

Best sound ever.

This time when she pulled him up, he let her take hold of him, and he entered her in one slow stroke, knowing there was no other place he wanted to be, no other person he wanted to do this with for the rest of his life.

She scooted closer and spread her legs wider, allowing him to sink further into her heat. Cupping her breasts, he teased her nipples with his thumbs, swallowing her moan with a deep kiss. He wanted to savor the sensations as he pulled out, only to have her tilt her hips and dig her nails into his ass before he slammed into her.

He felt her release build even as his own rushed forward. Then they were both coming and calling out each other's names. The perfect release with the perfect girl.

"I love you, Abby," he murmured against her mouth.

She sucked in air before pulling back and meeting his gaze. "I love you, Connor."

She bit her lip, and he caught a flicker of hesitation.

"What?" he asked, still buried deep inside her.

"I'm afraid of this. We've been here before. What if we can't make it work this time?"

A question he'd asked himself the past few days.

"I'd be lying if I didn't say I'm scared too." He lifted her chin to see eyes brimming with tears. "But I've learned sometimes you have to run toward what scares you."

"Like what you did to deal with your drug addiction."

"While this is a different kind of scary, the same principle applies. We talk openly and honestly about things, even if it makes us uncomfortable."

"Okay. What if I want to take things slow?" she said.

He pulled out a little before thrusting up, already feeling himself getting hard again. "I hope slow doesn't mean no more of this."

She laughed. "Connor Maguire, you are a sex addict."

"I can live with that, darlin'. Can you?"

"I'm offended you would think I couldn't handle your insatiable sexual appetite, mister."

She moved her hips, and he grew harder. He was more than halfway ready for round two.

She kneaded the muscles in his neck. "I meant we both have a lot going on right now. Me with my new business and you with yours. Let's enjoy this and work on building a relationship."

"I can do that." He caught her lips and kissed her deep. "I want you again."

"Really? I hadn't noticed," she teased, wrapping her legs around his back and pushing against the table until he took a few steps away.

"The thing is..." She pulled free of him. "You got your dessert, but I haven't gotten mine."

With a saucy smile, she hopped off the table and reached across the counter for the quart of chocolate marshmallow ice cream. From a drawer next to the sink, she extracted a spoon.

Removing the lid, she scooped a mouthful and sucked it into her mouth, licking the spoon in a suggestive way that practically had him falling on his knees.

Lucky spoon.

"Hop up." She patted the island.

He complied without hesitation. It was going to take all his strength to maintain control, but he was up for the task.

She finished the contents of the spoon and trailed it down his ribcage, stopping just below his belly button. Then she reloaded the spoon and gave him a sample before finishing the rest. Down she went, lower until she paused right over his erection, which was so hard that Connor thought it may break off.

Then the she-devil swallowed the cream and covered him with her cold lips. Connor cursed as she sucked him, the coldness from her mouth quickly heating him up. His resolve to not come too soon went out the window when she dipped a hand in the chocolate and proceeded to coat his cock, lapping the cold cream off with her tongue.

Her fingers worked his balls while her mouth did mind-blowing, torturous things to his cock until he couldn't hold on anymore.

"Fuck, Abby," he groaned as he held on to the side of the island and came in a rush that gave him a buzz more than he'd ever had when he was high.

Breathless, and even a little dizzy, he opened his eyes, watching as she swallowed and licked her way up his body until she got to his mouth.

"Best. Dessert. Ever," she said.

He clamped his mouth on hers, reveling in the taste of chocolate and himself on her tongue, intent on imprinting the memory of this moment in his mind forever.

"Definitely loved that," he said, and helped her onto the island with him. She straddled him and fed him a spoon of the now-soft ice cream.

"You're so beautiful, Abs." He kissed her, sharing his ice cream with her. "My beautiful seductress, lethal with a loaded spoon."

With his hands full of her breasts, he flicked her nipples, hearing the catch in her breath.

"You can't be ready again," she said.

Not yet, but soon.

He flipped her onto her back, pinning her arms over her head and taking control of the spoon.

With one hand restraining her hands, he dug into the container with the other hand and extracted a large spoonful, which he spread over her breasts.

She squealed.

He didn't stop.

He coated her and wished he could take a picture of her.

Aroused.

Breathless.

Covered in chocolate ice cream.

While his mouth explored and ate his fill, his free hand wandered down and slid inside her. She was drenched. He fed her ice cream from his mouth while seducing her with his hands until she trembled and cried out, thrashing against him.

Then he was inside her and, unable to stop, made love to her on the island until they both lay in a pool of chocolate, depleted and fully sated.

Abby rolled over, happily exhausted despite being up almost all night with Connor.

Showering off ice cream with Connor.

Talking, followed by more sex with Connor.

Being woken up for morning sex with Connor.

He was even more insatiable than he had been as a teen. And open for any suggestion and position.

And they'd gotten quite creative.

Especially on the kitchen island.

She pressed a kiss to his chest, loving the feel of waking in his arms. Why had she suggested they go slow when she could easily start every day like this?

"I think we should stay here all day," she said, burrowing into him.

He tightened his hold on her. "Wish I could, but Jace is already going to be ticked I blew off our morning meeting. I need to get to the lighthouse and supervise breaking ground on the museum."

"The permit came through?"

"Yesterday. We had our team on standby, so we can start today."

"Will this be filmed as part of the *Beach House Flippers*?"

"No. This is our own project."

Abby raised her head. "You mean you're paying for it?"

"The town council insisted on paying for the materials, but Jace and I are only charging them at cost, and we're paying the salaries."

She absently traced the dark circle around his nipple. "That's a nice thing to do."

"What's on your agenda today?"

"With the display shelves in the store all in place, Nat and I are going to stock them."

"I'll be pretty busy today and may not be able to stop by or touch base until late."

"No worries. You know where I am."

"I do." He kissed her long and tenderly. "Last night was amazing, darlin'."

"Just last night?" she teased, reaching between them to find him hard. Again.

"Last night and this morning." He pulled her hands away, kissing them. "And if you don't stop, I'll be late."

"How about a quick shower before you go?"

He took a peek at the clock on the bedside table. "It's going to have to be quick."

Abby watched his fine backside as he walked across the room to the bathroom.

He loved her. He'd spent the night telling and showing her how much.

Although it still frightened her a bit, she'd meant it when she told him she loved him too. Yet she was afraid something would ruin what they'd found. It was one thing to take chances with things like surfing or getting creative in the bedroom, but taking a risk with her heart or her career? Not as easy.

She'd struggled since Hurricane Samantha, waiting to start college until a couple of years after the storm. Once she graduated and got a job, she'd stayed at the cosmetic company in Texas longer than she wanted and procrastinated taking a chance on the soap shop.

And now here she was, naked and getting ready for another round of morning sex with Connor. And only a few days away from the grand opening of her place. She was afraid the house of cards she'd built would come toppling down.

"I'm starting without you, darlin'," Connor called from the bathroom.

Brushing aside her worries, she joined him.

Fifteen minutes later, she emerged clean and thoroughly ravished. With her hair damp, she tugged on clothes and went to fix Connor a cup of coffee to bring with him.

Abby walked into the kitchen and stopped short at the disaster before her. The island streaked with ice cream, the container—empty—on its side along with the spoon, and clothes strewn all over the room. Connor's tan shorts and boxer briefs had taken the brunt of the mess and sat in a pile on the floor where chocolate had dripped on them. She picked them up and set them next to the sink to rinse them out before washing them.

Despite the mess, Abby smiled at the memory of their night. It topped her list of erotic food exploits, for sure. After starting a pot of coffee, she reached into a cabinet to get a mug, but it slipped out of her hands and fell, shattering with a loud crash.

"Abs? You okay?" Connor called.

"Yeah. I dropped a coffee mug."

She picked up the bigger pieces and was tossing them in the trash when Connor came in, freshly dressed for work.

"Wow, we did a number on your kitchen." He planted a soft kiss on her lips. "Best night of my life."

"Mine too."

"Let me help you clean up this glass. You have a dustpan?"

"In the closet in the corner."

While Connor searched, Abby grabbed a takeout mug and fixed the coffee the way he liked. When he hadn't returned, she called out. "You find it, babe?"

She found him in the closet fixated on something in the back.

"What's that?" he asked, and his voice held an edge that sent a shiver down her spine.

"What? The dustpan's right here." She reached past him to where it was on the shelf, pausing when she saw what had caught his eye.

In the corner, partially hidden behind a bucket and mop, were several cans of spray paint. Someone had done a poor job of trying to cover them up with a couple of old towels.

She wrinkled her brow. "I've never seen those before."

"They're the same color as the paint used when Erickson Pier was vandalized. And at both the mini-golf and the museum sites," Connor said.

"It's probably common spray paint. Most likely from the past owner," Abby said, not liking the accusatory tone in his voice.

"But then there's this." He held out a newspaper. It was the front page of an old issue of the *Pelican Bay Herald* and covered an article about the renovation of Erickson Pier and the filming of *Beach House Flippers*. In the margin, someone had written the words *GO HOME*.

Abby remembered Connor mentioning similar wording being painted at the lighthouse.

"Oh my God. You think *I'm* responsible for the vandalism?"

He raised pained eyes to her. "Do you know how these things got here?"

"I just told you I don't. Does that make me guilty?"

"You organized the protest about the pier expansion, Abby. You have to admit it's a strange coincidence to find this in your apartment."

"You have some nerve." She stomped into the kitchen, wincing when she stepped on particles of glass she'd forgotten about.

"Dammit." Hopping on one foot, she moved to the counter and bent over to pull out shards of glass.

Connor had followed her. "Fuck. The glass."

He disappeared into the pantry and returned with the dustpan and brush to sweep up the pieces.

Abby thought about the past couple of months. Sure, she'd been pretty peeved when she learned the Ericksons were going to expand the pier and block her store's view of the beach. The view was the main reason she'd chosen the location for her shop. Only after signing a two-year lease did she fully grasp the extent of the renovation.

And sure, she'd banded together with the Egg Harbor Beach Preservation Group, who helped her understand her rights and proposed protesting with a few other business owners to make their point.

But for Connor to think she'd break into the pier while it was being renovated, destroy property, and paint childish words was beyond ridiculous.

It was insulting.

"Here." Connor put something in her hand. "Put this wet paper towel on your foot."

"Fuck my damn toe." She pushed away. "Do you really think I'm capable of vandalism?"

He shook his head. "No."

"Then why did you practically accuse me?"

He ran a hand through his hair. "I'm sorry. I found the paint in there, and it seemed an odd coincidence you'd have paint the same color. Then I saw the newspaper article, and I didn't know what to think."

"So, you assumed the worst of me?"

"It wasn't like that."

Except it was completely like that.

"You're supposed to believe in me. How can we build a relationship if you think I'm capable of something like this?"

"Abby, I didn't think. I just spoke. I'm an ass."

She crossed her arms. "No argument there."

She racked her brain but couldn't for the life of her figure out where the paint had come from. Could Natalie be involved?

"I think you should call the cops," Connor said.

"The cops?" Abby shrieked.

"Let Ethan know. He's been gathering evidence on the other vandalism. He told me when I dropped off the necklace I found."

"What necklace?"

"I didn't tell you? I found it at the museum site yesterday. A stainless-steel chain with a baseball charm on it."

Abby's blood ran cold.

Connor continued, "Oh, and the letter P, for the Phillies, on the baseball."

No, no, no. It can't be. Not sweet Liam. Please no.

Abby remembered Liam got caught a couple of days ago smoking a joint at the mini-golf place. Had he and his friends been working their way through the town, playing childish pranks?

Connor's cell dinged with a text. "Fuck, I'm late."

"You should go. I'll clean this up," Abby said.

"What about the paint?"

"I'll deal with it, and call Ethan."

"And what about us?"

"I don't know, Connor. I need to think," she said, unable to keep the hurt and anger out of her tone.

"I'll come over after work, and we'll talk. I don't want this to mess us up." He came over and kissed her. "I love you, Abby."

She closed her eyes. "I know you do."

Another kiss, and he was gone.

Abby placed her face in her hands.

If only you could trust me, too.

Chapter Eleven

CONNOR REMOVED HIS HARD hat and used the back of his hand to wipe away the sweat on his brow. The construction crew they'd hired was on a lunch break, and he removed his earplugs before taking a swig of water. They'd made decent progress digging the hole for the foundation of the museum.

Unfortunately, no amount of digging or the distraction of needing to answer a million questions could take Connor's mind off what happened over the past twenty-four hours with Abby.

First had been the mind-blowing sex. They'd always had an active and creative sex life, but last night put their past escapades to shame.

The intimacy went beyond satisfying their physical need.

He'd told Abby he loved her, and she said it back.

She loved him.

He wanted to shout it from the top of the lighthouse.

Except overshadowing the joy of hearing her admit her feelings was the way they'd ended things earlier.

The last thing Connor had expected was to find orange spray paint cans and the newspaper article in Abby's closet.

Had he handled it right by basically accusing her of being responsible for the vandalism?

Not at all.

In his defense, given the paint and newspaper were discovered in Abby's apartment, it was natural to wonder if there could be a link to the vandalism. At least indirectly connected, in Connor's opinion.

Could she blame him for jumping to conclusions? Abby had made a huge fuss about the pier expansion. Enough to draw attention from the media and cause the foundation team, mayor, and town council to consider other options to avoid further problems and bad press.

Still, what did it say about his opinion of her—of their relationship—that he, for even a moment, thought her capable of something illegal?

And now what? Had he blown his chance with her?

Meanwhile, if Abby hadn't put the paper and paint in her closet, who had? Could Natalie be responsible? How about Abby's nephew? Hadn't she said Liam had been getting into trouble? The necklace Connor found was something a young boy would wear.

Frustrated, he walked along the rocks that bordered the lighthouse. From early childhood, it had been a favorite place to hang out. He used to take stale bread—when there was any—and feed the pelicans. There was a group who used to populate this portion of the island. One in particular had a distinctive scar on his bill, and Connor and his friends had named him Percy. He and the rest of the pelicans disappeared after Hurricane Samantha.

Hopefully, creating the nature trail would attract pelicans and other wildlife to the island. But until the vandals were caught, Connor hesitated to put forth more effort in building the trail.

Which led him back to his dilemma with Abby.

"Hey, bro," Jason said as he made his way across the rocks. "Nice day for digging."

Connor caught the wrapped sandwich his brother tossed him. "Yeah, perfect conditions. We keep up this pace and we should have the foundation dug in a couple of days."

They ate in silence, the only interruption from the faint sound of music in the background, the waves crashing against the rocks, and a few seagulls circling overhead.

"You want to tell me what's wrong?" Jason asked.

"Nothing's wrong."

Jason balled up the wrapper from his sandwich and threw it in the bag. "You blew off our morning meeting and were thirty minutes late getting here. And I can tell by your cranky disposition it's not for a good reason."

One of the frustrating things about having lived in a small space with someone was the lack of privacy. Jason and he had shared a room their entire lives until they bought the townhouse in Tampa. Which meant Jason knew firsthand the good, the bad, and the ugly of Connor's moods. And vice versa.

"Last night, I told Abby I love her," Connor said.

"I'm not surprised, but admitting it...Wow. Does she feel the same way?"

"She does...or she did. I'm not sure how she feels anymore."

"What happened?"

Connor sighed and set aside his half-eaten sandwich. "I was helping her clean up a mug she broke and was looking for a dustpan in a closet. I found three cans of fluorescent orange spray paint and a newspaper article about us renovating Erickson Pier."

"Coincidence?"

"You tell me. The paper had the words *GO HOME* written in the margin."

Jason winced. "What'd you do?"

"I asked her where it came from. She claims to have never seen it there before."

"Do you believe her?"

"I believe Abby wasn't responsible for the vandalism. That was after I all but accused her of it."

"Not good, bro."

"No shit." Connor picked up a pebble and pitched it into the ocean. "How did the stuff get there? There has to be a connection to the string of vandalism."

"You think Natalie is responsible?"

Connor shrugged. "Maybe. Didn't you catch her son smoking at mini-golf?"

"I did, but it doesn't mean he's involved," Jason said.

"How about the necklace I found? It was a cheap trinket...something a boy would wear."

"You mention it to Abby?"

"I mentioned finding it just before your text came through and I left." Connor thought about their conversation. Had she seemed paler than usual when he described the necklace, or had it been his imagination?

"I don't know, man. You call Ethan?"

"She was going to."

She needed to call Ethan in order for it not to appear as though she was hiding evidence. If she was innocent and protecting the real culprit, it was as bad as doing it herself, in Connor's mind.

And if that was the case, Connor didn't know what it meant to their relationship.

After Connor left, Abby had cleaned up the kitchen, and now paced the back room of the soap shop. She had made more soap samples last night and left them out to set. Now, rather than wrapping them like she should do, she was trying to figure out the best way to approach her sister and ask if her son could be responsible for the vandalism.

She texted Ethan and asked him to come over around nine thirty, which would give her and Nat a chance to talk first. Plus, it prevented Abby from wimping out and not turning over potential evidence...or Nat convincing her not to.

They had to tell Ethan.

Regardless of how the paint and newspaper got in her closet, Abby didn't see any way they weren't connected to the vandalism.

Her integrity and business relied on her doing the right thing.

Not to mention her relationship with Connor.

His eyes had been cold when he asked her about the paint cans. Had he believed she could be responsible for the vandalism around town?

Could she be with a man who could think that about her?

And what about the necklace Connor found at the museum site? Based on the description, it sounded exactly like the one Liam owned.

What if Liam was responsible for the vandalism? How would it affect her family? Her business?

The rattle of the door handle got her attention, and Natalie pushed open the door, carrying a large box and a plastic recycled grocery bag.

"Morning. I picked up the baskets from Emma and other decorations like we talked about," she said, setting the items on the floor. "I'm excited to organize the main room displays today."

"We need to talk first."

Natalie wrinkled her brow. "What's wrong? Did you and Connor get into a fight?"

Abby took a deep breath like she did before jumping into a pool. "Connor found something in the closet off the kitchen upstairs."

"Okay, what did he find that has you rattled?"

"Orange fluorescent spray paint cans and a *Pelican Bay Herald* featuring the article about *Beach House Flippers* renovating Erickson Pier."

"That's weird," Natalie said.

"Someone had written *GO HOME* in the margin."

Abby could see Natalie processing, and her eyes widened when she realized what conclusions had been drawn. "Please tell me he doesn't think you were responsible for the vandalism at the pier."

"There's been vandalism all over town. Several other Maguire Brothers properties have had similar words painted in the same color. Even the area by the lighthouse, where they marked off the location for the museum, was affected."

"Is he accusing you of being involved? If so, then he's an ass and not worthy of you."

"The thing is, Nat, he found something at the lighthouse. Something that worries me."

"What?"

Abby reached across the counter for a framed photo she kept on a table in her living room and set it in front of her sister. It was of Abby, Natalie, Liam, Olivia, and their mom taken at Christmas last year.

"Connor found a necklace at the museum site." She pointed to the chain Liam wore in the picture. "And based on his description, it matches this one."

Natalie scoffed, but picked up the picture. "Jake gave this to Liam for his birthday last summer. They'd gone to a Phillies game, and he bought Liam this pendant to remember their day together."

"I remember. He never takes it off. Have you seen him wear it recently?"

"I'm not sure. I yelled at him the other day because he trashed his room."

"Could he have been searching for the necklace, not realizing where he lost it?"

"It's possible." Natalie put her hand over her mouth. "What if it is him, Ab? Ethan has been all over this vandalism case. What if my son is responsible?"

Abby put an arm around her sister. "I don't know what to believe, but I think it's possible Liam and his band of friends may somehow be involved."

There was a knock at the door.

Ethan.

Now they'd have to tell the story to him and hope they were wrong, or there was a reasonable explanation for Liam's odd behavior.

But something told Abby the odds wouldn't be in their favor.

Either way, she owed Connor an apology for getting angry at him for jumping to conclusions. Even though she wasn't responsible for the vandalism, Connor wasn't that far off the mark. If he hadn't had to rush off, they could have figured it out together. But she'd gotten angry, and he had to get to the job site.

Would he understand, or would their relationship be ruined just when they'd found their way back to each other?

Chapter Twelve

ABBY DRUMMED HER FINGERS on the steering wheel of her vintage Orange-Crush-colored Jeep Wrangler. After texting and calling Connor multiple times throughout the afternoon with no response, she'd packed a picnic dinner and taken a chance he'd be at his apartment.

No luck there, either. The inside of Maguire Brothers Renovations was also dark, so Jenna and Jason must have left for the day. It was almost seven. Maybe Connor had gone to Emma's for dinner.

She sent her friend a text and received a response that Connor wasn't there.

That morning, Connor had said something about breaking ground today on the property for the museum. Could he still be there?

Only one way to find out.

Abby put the Jeep into drive and headed toward the lighthouse. The parking lot was blockaded off, probably because of the construction. A dumpster, port-a-john, and several large construction vehicles stood parked in an area gated off with plastic fencing.

She was about to drive away when she caught sight of a dark gray truck parked by the dunes past the lighthouse entrance.

Connor's truck.

After pulling up her car behind his, she grabbed the picnic basket and went in search of him. She found him on the water, paddling out on his board way past where the waves broke.

He straddled the board with his back to her and watched the horizon. His wide shoulders exuded strength and skill. With a sudden turn, he rolled onto his stomach and paddled toward shore, popping up with an effortless grace she'd never attain, even with all the lessons he'd given her when they were kids. As he rode the wave in, she studied his tall frame, the confident stance and perfect balance on the board. His shaggy hair framed his face in a wild tangle.

God, she loved him.

She'd spent the past decade going to school, working, doing whatever she could to forget about her past on Pelican Bay, and her love for the boy who left her.

Moving back had been a decision she'd made for herself. Not because of obligation, but because she wasn't happy in Texas or working for the large cosmetics firm. She'd wanted a different life...on her terms. And she'd missed her family.

Her decision to make the move permanently happened the moment she opened her car door and smelled the salt air. She knew she'd come home and was there to stay.

Now she was preparing to launch a new career...her own business. If only she could figure out how to keep the guy this time.

Having walked close to the water, she spread out the blanket she'd brought near a backpack she recognized as Connor's. After kicking off her sandals, she continued to watch Connor surf, knowing she'd never tire of the view.

Of the beach.

Of the man.

Finally, Connor walked out of the ocean, the board under his arm. He stopped a few feet from her and set the board down in the sand.

She eyed him warily. "Good waves?"

He grabbed a beach towel out of his bag and dried off his hair and face. "Not bad."

"I texted and called you a few times today."

"My cell wasn't fully charged and died halfway through the morning."

Was he really going to pull that with her?

"Portable chargers come in handy, especially when you're working on a construction site."

He didn't respond, and after removing his wetsuit, he set it on the board to dry. Underneath, he wore navy board shorts, and he slipped a dark gray T-shirt over his head.

She handed him a bottle of water. "Have you eaten? I brought dinner."

"Thanks. No, I haven't." He chugged half the contents.

"Can we talk first?"

He dropped onto the blanket next to her. "I don't know what to say. I don't want to fight."

"Then let's not fight. Let's talk." She scooted closer to him. "If we're going to be in a relationship, there will be times we'll tick each other off. We may even raise our voices at each other."

"I know, it's just..." He angled his head toward the sea. "I went to an NA support meeting this afternoon."

"Oh. I wondered if you went to meetings regularly."

"I go weekly. It keeps me in check, and I can offer help to others who are in the early stages of dealing with their drug addiction," he said. "I was feeling anxious and stressed and needed to talk with others who understand."

"You were stressed about our fight."

"About the fight, about the vandalism, about my dad wanting to remarry my mom, about starting a serious relationship with you."

"That's a lot to be stressed about," she said.

He snorted. "Tell me about it."

"Did it help?"

"It did." He turned to face her. "I'm sorry for how I reacted to finding the paint cans. I jumped to conclusions and assumed the worst."

"You had valid points. I was a real bitch about the pier extension and could have handled it better. I can see how finding the paint cans in my closet could raise suspicion."

He nodded and turned to the ocean. "After the meeting, I came here to surf. Helps clear my mind."

"I can see why."

He met her eyes again. "Going to meetings will always be a part of my life. I need to know you can accept me, flaws and all."

She reached for his hand. "I know who you are, flaws and all. It's not like I'm perfect. You know I have my own issues. I'm impatient. I get angry quickly."

"You're stubborn."

"A flaw we both have in common."

He laughed. "We do. Can we make this work, Abby?"

The yearning behind his question touched her heart.

"I think we owe it to ourselves to try." She cupped his whisker-covered jaw. "I love you, Connor, and will do everything I can to make this work."

"I love you, Abby, and I want to build a life with you."

"Then let's promise to make each other a priority. And talk through what we're feeling, even when we're angry with each other."

"I can do that."

"I can come to your meetings with you. Not sure it's allowed, but I want to understand and support you however I can."

His eyes filled, and he leaned his head against hers. "Darlin', you're supporting me by offering. Sometimes we can bring a relative, spouse, or girlfriend to a meeting. I'll let you know when."

"Sounds good. Con, can you kiss me now?"

He framed her face and pressed a soft kiss against her lips. She opened and let him in, their tongues caressing and seeking love and forgiveness.

She threw her arms around him and buried her face in his neck. "I hate fighting, too, but we're going to have some pretty fantastic make-up sex."

"That's a fact, although it will take something pretty spectacular to top last night." He glanced up at the lighthouse. "Let's eat. I have an idea on how."

They ate a dinner of cold roasted chicken and chickpea salad. Connor listened while Abby updated him on her conversation with Natalie.

"Has Natalie talked to Liam about the paint cans and necklace?" he asked.

"She's been trying to find him. He stayed overnight at a friend's house and was supposed to work at Harrison's this afternoon, but didn't show up. And he's not answering her texts or calls."

Connor remembered the creative ways he'd found to avoid going home some nights, including staying at a friend's house, telling his mom he was working late, or even sometimes sleeping on the beach. Anything to allow him to party into oblivion.

"What did Ethan say?"

"He listened to what happened and collected the cans and newspaper. It was uncomfortable, since he and Nat have been seeing each other, or at least sleeping together."

"Ouch. Yeah, this makes things a little weird."

"I don't understand why Liam would act out this way."

"Didn't you say he was hanging out with a new group of friends?"

"Yeah, they're the ones Jason caught smoking pot a few nights ago. I still can't wrap my head around that."

Connor could appreciate it being difficult for an adult to believe the worst about someone they'd known since birth.

Still, it didn't negate the truth and the cold, hard facts.

"I tried my first joint at twelve and was dealing by fourteen," Connor said. "It happens. I wish my mom would have found out and stopped me. But with working three jobs, we barely saw her."

"This is Nat's last week working at the five and dime, and she's only working a few shifts on the weekend at Tonino's, with the shop opening."

Giving Liam lots of time on his own...at a vulnerable age.

"Starting a business is going to be hard on both of you. Stores here stay open late during tourist season. The more she's away, the more trouble Liam can get into."

Abby frowned. "You're right. Nat's been focused on saving money, hoping she can get her own place instead of living with our mom. Plus, she's trying to put away money for Liam to go to college."

"There's community college and other lower-cost options in Jersey to consider. And if Liam keeps getting into trouble, it will make getting into college harder," Connor said.

"She and I have had similar conversations. Honestly, I'm not sure what she's thinking." Abby closed up the containers and stored them in the cooler. "Right now, we need to get through the store opening, but Nat may be forced to deal with whatever trouble Liam has gotten into sooner than later."

Something had been on his mind, and he hoped Abby wouldn't get angry if he poked his nose into her business more than he already had.

"Have you considered hiring a couple part-time workers? You'll have to continue to make inventory, and with only you and Natalie, it will make it hard to cover all the hours."

"It's funny you ask. I took out an ad yesterday. I got a couple of calls today and scheduled two interviews tomorrow," she said.

"Good to hear, darlin'." He pushed her hair aside and kissed her neck, inhaling the scent of daisies and sunshine. "I hear you have a demanding boyfriend who will be lonely if you're not home every night until late."

She laughed. "I'll work out a schedule so I can give plenty of attention to my demanding boyfriend."

"He would be appreciative, but I suppose he'll understand and can use the time for non-work projects."

"He sounds like a nice guy." She turned and snuggled into his neck.

"Hey, no sleeping."

She yawned. "Sorry, someone kept me up most of the night last night."

"Speaking of up...I have an idea."

"What?"

"I'm told there's an amazing view of the sun setting over the bay from the top of the lighthouse. You up for climbing stairs?"

"My ankle is almost better, so sure."

Connor stowed his board and Abby's cooler in his truck, grabbed a flashlight, and met her at the door to the lighthouse.

He extracted a key from his pocket and inserted it into the old lock.

"Where did you get the key from?" she asked.

"Jason gave it to me. Emma's family still had the key from when Jace used to take care of the grounds here as a teen. He used to come here with Emma when they wanted to get away from everything."

"Translation: they used to have sex here."

He laughed. "Probably, although I don't want to think about what they did here now...or ever."

He wiggled the key and pressed a shoulder against the old door, pleased when it gave way and opened with a creak.

"Is it safe?" Abby asked, a little worry in her tone.

"I went up there the other day and checked it out. Swept away dirt and bugs."

Abby pressed against him. "Bugs?"

He was going to enjoy this.

"Hurry or we'll miss the sunset."

He turned on the flashlight and shined the bright light on the stairs. Taking her hand in his, he headed up the steep climb.

Two hundred and eleven steps later, they made it to the top landing.

"Well, I got in my exercise for the week," Abby said, slightly winded.

"It will be worth it. I promise."

Connor led her over to the side where the windows faced the bay. The sun had started dipping. A colorful kaleidoscope of yellow, red, and purple reflected off the water.

Abby sucked in her breath. "It's beautiful."

Connor bent and flicked on the battery-operated string lights he'd bought earlier, along with a couple of flameless candles, and shut off the flashlight.

With Abby in front of him, his arms curled around her waist, they watched the colors change as the sun dropped lower and lower below the horizon.

Connor could stay like this forever. A town and job he loved, surrounded by friends and family, and now with his girl. Abby was his soul mate, and holding her in his arms was the perfect end to a stressful day.

"Thanks for sharing this with me," she said.

"Next time, we'll go out to the dock. But there we can't do this." He spun her and kissed her, a slow, seductive kiss that quickly grew hot until he pulled away to catch his breath.

Picking up the blanket Abby brought with her, he spread it out on the floor.

"You're not kidding? We're going to do this here?"

He pulled her close, sliding his hands down her breasts, along her ribs and stomach, stopping a moment before they slipped under her dress. Her breath caught as he trailed a finger against the silk of her panties, feeling the dampness and heat.

"Most definitely," he said, his voice husky.

She shuddered and pressed closer to him. He lifted the dress over her head until she stood bathed in candlelight in her bra and thong.

Beautiful.

Mine.

Fingering the straps of her bra, he slid them down, bending over to capture an exposed nipple. With a flick of his fingers, the clasp opened, and it fell to the floor. He kissed his way down her body, taking time with her breasts, sucking her nipple into his mouth until her breathing was raspy.

Dropping to his knees, he ran his fingers under the waistband of her panties and slid them down her legs. He could smell her arousal, and the heady scent made him even harder. He kissed her mound, feeling her part her legs for him to explore.

She held on to his shoulders for support, her head thrown back as she fought for control. Only Connor *wanted* her to lose control. He inserted a finger and curled it up while sucking her clit. Her legs started shaking, and when he added a second digit inside, he held her up while she cried out and came.

Sweating, he yanked his shirt off and fumbled with the tie to his shorts. When he was naked, he helped her to the ground.

He had bought a few outdoor pillows and arranged them under her head.

When she took his cock in hand, he sucked in a breath. Hovering over her, he let her guide him into her, taking it slow even though he could tell by her insistent hands that she wanted to go fast.

He kissed the curve of her neck, moving to her mouth. "Love you so much, Abby."

She arched her hips up and pushed on his ass. "Love you, Connor. But you're killing me now."

"Am I?" He pulled all the way out, cupping her breasts and tugging at her nipples.

She moaned. "You're evil."

"In the best possible way, darlin'."

He slammed into her and quickened the pace until they were both bathed in sweat and calling out their release together.

Despite the heat and lack of air circulation, they lay curled together.

Connor had started to doze when Abby nudged him in the side. "Did you hear that? I hear a noise outside."

From below came the sound of scraping along with the indistinct murmur of voices.

Male voices.

Jumping awake, he sat up, reaching for his clothes and straining to make out the words.

Abby turned off the candles after dressing and crouched by the window. She scurried away and whispered in his ear, "I think it's Liam and a couple of other boys."

"Back for round two?"

"They have shovels and flashlights. I think they're searching for something."

"Liam's necklace."

Abby nodded. "What do we do?"

Connor already had his cell phone out and was typing. "I'm texting Ethan."

"Should I text Natalie?"

"Not yet. Let Ethan do his thing." He moved to the window, staying to the side, where he was in the shadows. "I'm going to take a little video."

Less than five minutes later, a loud, piercing siren broke the silence, followed by the bright headlights of Ethan's vehicle as it screeched to a halt in the parking lot. Connor heard cursing as the boys abandoned the shovels and tried to scurry away. But Ethan and his partner were quick and had them surrounded.

"Let's go," Connor said, turning on his flashlight before starting down the stairs.

Abby followed behind him.

Outside, they made their way to the construction site to see Ethan leading the boys to the back of his SUV. They walked single file. The first with his head down, the second wiping his eyes, and the third yelling that his father would have their badge.

Ethan jogged over. "Thanks for the call. Didn't catch them with any spray cans, though."

"What the hell were they doing? We saw them digging," Connor said.

"Seems they were looking for the necklace Liam lost," Ethan said.

"Busted at the scene of the crime," Connor said. "Good for us, bad for them."

"Can I talk to Liam?" Abby asked.

"Make it quick. I'm going to call Natalie and let her know we're taking them to the station," Ethan said.

"You're going to put them in jail?" Abby cried.

Connor put an arm around her shoulder. "It'll be all right, Abs. Let Ethan do his job."

"I won't put them in a cell, but I need to ask them questions about the vandalism," Ethan said.

Connor and Ethan hung back while she ran over to Liam.

"Kind of ironic that you, a delinquent when we were kids, busted the minor of the woman you're sleeping with," Connor said.

Ethan rubbed the back of his neck. "Irony sucks. Nat's going to hate me for taking him to the station."

"You have to do your job, man."

"You know it's not going to matter to her." Ethan watched as his deputy helped the boys into the squad car. "I've tried to get to know the kid, but Nat hasn't wanted to tell him about us."

Connor snorted. "She's using you for sex. Again, there's that irony."

"Yeah," Ethan said with a sad shake of his head.

"You thinking community service?"

"Hard to say. We didn't catch them vandalizing, and I'm not sure the spray paint you found will prove they were responsible for any of the incidents."

"If you need them to do a little community work, I could use a few kids who know how to use a shovel to help with the nature trail," Connor said.

Ethan clapped him on the shoulder. "I'll keep it in mind." He took out his phone. "Let me make this call to Nat."

"Good luck."

Abby returned, her face streaked with tears.

"Come here, darlin'." Connor pulled her close and let her cry.

"He's so frustrating...angry at the world. I don't know how to help him," she said.

Sometimes people have to make their own mistakes and learn life lessons the hard way.

Just like Connor had.

"Has anything changed in his life?"

Abby sniffed. "His dad is expecting a baby with another woman. They're getting married this fall."

Bingo.

"If Liam thinks his dad doesn't have time for him, he could act out for attention or to make a point."

"What kind of point? That Nat can't handle him?"

Connor shrugged. "Possibly. Think about it. If Nat can't control Liam, and he keeps getting into trouble, she may send him to live with his dad."

"Nat mentioned the possibility of alternative living arrangements for Liam after the summer ends. It was an offhand comment, though. Not sure she'd really send him away."

"See, his plan—assuming that's his goal—may already be working."

They watched as Ethan got in the car and they took off.

"I guess you have a valid point." She rested her head on his shoulder. "For the most part we grew up without a dad. But he died. It's not like he was an hour away. It's been a struggle for Nat trying to juggle everything."

"Understandable. I'm sure she'll figure it out. We'll support her with whatever she needs."

"You don't need to take this on. It's my family."

"And we're dating, which means it's important to me, too." He kissed her. "And in case I'm not being clear enough, I'm talking forever, Abby. I want marriage and kids...with you."

"Is that a marriage proposal?"

"I wasn't sure you wanted to go there this soon. You wanted to take things slow."

She wrapped her arms around him. "When have we ever done anything slow?"

She had him there.

He reached for her left hand and kissed it. "Abby O'Connell, what do you say we act like grownups and get hitched?"

"I say it's about damned time, Connor Maguire."

Epilogue

ABBY AND NATALIE STOOD next to Mayor John and posed for the camera before cutting the ribbon in front of their new store. That, along with a loud cheer from the crowd gathered on the boardwalk, and Soap Sisters was officially open for business.

Friends and family filled the store, oohing and aahing over the displays. After some heated deliberation, Abby and Natalie had settled on a beach theme decor. The primary display was a mermaid statue Maddy had found with help from Emma. Connor and Jason had built a rock platform, complete with actual running water. The mermaid sat perched on the rocks with various soaps in dishes all along the rocks. Soap shaped like fish and frogs sat in boats and on lily pads.

They'd kept the mermaid theme throughout the store and added shells and treasure chests with soaps inside.

The two women they'd hired had been godsends. They were quick to learn the sales app Maddy helped them set up, and more than willing to learn about the products. They even had suggestions and ideas for other displays, which were incorporated. One of the women's sisters made jewelry out of sea glass. Abby asked if she could contact her about selling a few items on consignment. It was good to grow and support other local businesses.

The coupons they had handed out with the sample soaps had been a hit and, along with the ads and other marketing, enticed customers to the store. They had a steady stream of people all day, and it wasn't until late afternoon that Abby found a moment to slip into the back and grab more stock. At this rate, she'd have to step up her production sooner than she'd expected.

A definite win from her perspective.

Warm arms circled her waist. "Hey, pretty darlin'. How's my favorite business owner?" Connor pressed a kiss to her neck.

"Exhausted, but happy. People are coming and buying stuff."

"Why do you sound surprised?"

"I've worried and stressed about it for so long that it's hard to believe it's happening."

"Well, it is, and I couldn't be prouder of you. I'm especially excited to try out the massage oil I bought, although I was disappointed it wasn't edible."

She laughed. "It's not *that* kind of store. And you don't need to pay. You are engaged to one of the owners."

"Speaking of which." He reached into his pocket. "I was going to wait until later, but I've never been good at holding back surprises."

Abby's heart pounded as he dropped to one knee.

"Abby O'Connell, let's make this official. I want to spend all of my days and nights with you for the rest of our lives. Will you make an honest man out of me and marry me?"

She looked at the gorgeous man who held up an enormous princess-cut diamond ring and knew they'd make it work. Sure, there would be ups and downs, but any day with Connor was a good day. Abby would never doubt their love again, and would spend the rest of her life showing and telling him.

"I've only ever needed you, Connor. I'll be the happiest woman to be your wife." She held out her ring finger, and he slipped it on.

"Love you so much, my sweet Abby," he said.

"Love you more."

They shared a tender kiss that spoke of love and forever.

Connor waggled his eyebrows. "Think they'll miss the boss for thirty minutes?"

She pushed him toward the stairs. "I think they'll be just fine."

Life with Connor was going to be exciting, full of passion, adventure, and love.

She couldn't wait another minute for it to start.

MORE PELICAN BAY!

I hope you enjoyed reading Connor and Abby's story! Would you be kind enough to post a short review on Goodreads, BookBub, or your retailer? Reviews help future readers find a new book to enjoy! Thanks so much!

Was this your first Pelican Bay story? If so, be sure to read Emma and Jason's story in *You're Still the One*, available now on Amazon. Tempted by a chance to renovate the amusement pier in his hometown as part of his reality TV show, Jason agrees to return, even though it will mean working closely with Emma, who once broke his heart. Now, they'll need to work together to attract new tourists to the dying beach town. Can they overcome their past and make a new beginning?

There's more to come. You can return to Pelican Bay in *A Kiss in the Moonlight*...coming soon!

Subscribe to my newsletter at mariakalexander.com for cover reveal, release date, sneak peaks, and more! Sign up and receive a free digital copy of *Till There Was You*, a prequel to the Pelican Bay series!

If you prefer to only receive new release alerts, please follow me on Book-Bub or Amazon.

Awaken My Heart (Tangled Hearts Book 3)

One unforgettable night...a lie that can cost them everything.
Lies have a way of coming back to haunt you—a lesson Ashley O'Neil learns the hard way when she runs into the man she shared a steamy night with years ago. Now, tangled in a web of deception, she'll need to right a wrong and chance losing her heart to the very man she deceived. When Detective Nick DiFrancesco's drug trafficking case goes south, a lead puts him in Ashley's path. With his family in danger and his heart on the line, he'll need to fight for justice and risk it all to a woman he's never forgotten.

Believe in My Heart (Tangled Hearts Book 4)

This holiday season, love is on the menu.
Culinary arts student and event coordinator, Hope Mastriano, is down on her luck. Homeless on Thanksgiving Day, she's caught trying to break into her cousin's apartment by her sexy boss and lifelong secret crush. After getting dumped seven months ago, head chef Vinnie DiFrancesco's life is sent into a tailspin when he offers Hope temporary housing. With the trattoria's Italian Christmas Eve charity dinner to be featured on a local TV segment and things heating up in his apartment, the two must set aside their different visions to secure the future of the restaurant and make it a Christmas to remember.

Acknowledgments

I'm extremely grateful to share this book with you. Connor and Abby's story literally flew out of me! I'm blessed with a wonderful family that supports my writing. Many thanks to my beta readers, Tina Gabrielle, RoseAnn DeFranco, and Jessica Ketterer for your time and thoughtful comments. A shout out to my editing team, Arran McNicol and Jen Coleman, and my wonderful cover designer, Lyndsey Lewellen at LLewellen Designs.com for a beautiful cover.

With each book in the Pelican Bay series, I strive to bring you a little bit more of the fictional town that combines elements of my favorite beach towns along the Jersey shore. I hope you feel that love in the stories and enjoy getting to know the characters. As always, thanks to my readers for your continued support!

About the Author

Maria K. Alexander is an award-winning author of the Tangled Hearts series. She writes about women who are fearless in pursuit of their ambitions. Her stories have strong connections with family and friends. When not writing, she loves to read, bake, crochet, bike, visit the beach, and watch romantic comedies. She lives in New Jersey with her husband and juggles a full-time job. To connect with Maria or learn more about her books, please visit:

www.mariakalexander.com